Massacre at the Citadel

Massacre at the Citadel

Said Magdi

Cover image: Painting by David Ashraf, Alexandria, Egypt.

To my children

Author's Note

A Mameluke is described in The Tormont Webster's Illustrated Encyclopedic Dictionary as:

> A member of a former military cast, originally composed of slaves from Turkey, that held the Egyptian throne from about 1250 until 1517 and remained in power until 1811.

The Mamelukes remained powerful until they were deliberately massacred at the Citadel by order of Mohammed Ali Pasha, who had been appointed governor of Egypt by the Ottoman Sultan. Undoubtedly, the fact that the creators of a dominant empire could simply be slaughtered in a matter of days is horrifying. Although many historians view Mohammed Ali as the *Father of Modern Egypt*, others hold the view that only his personal ruthless ambition and greed were the primary guiding forces in modernizing Egypt.

Massacre at the Citadel is a work of fiction that embraces the legend of the one Mameluke who, many still believe to this day, had managed to escape the gruesome carnage. It also includes other events and adventures and invites readers to visit life in Cairo at that time.

Special thanks to Ardèle Warr, Louse-Nicole Dupuy, and Marie Anne McGarr as first readers, and to Jean Seville Suffield as editor. Their help in making this novel come to life is very much appreciated. I also wish to express my gratitude to David Ashraf, Architect, for his creative artistic painting of the massacre. Undoubtedly, it has helped significantly in designing the book cover.

Prologue

*E*_{*gypt*} *is the gift of the Nile,* so affirmed the Greek historian Herodotus describing Egypt in the fifth century BC. Obviously, the statement is true since without the Nile, Egypt would have been a harsh arid desert. For countless millennia, the river Nile leisurely streamed from central Africa northward, generously spreading life and prosperity over many barren regions before ending its long journey into the Mediterranean Sea. One of the earliest known civilizations was founded on its banks by the Pharaohs. The Pyramids and Sphinx are just a few examples of testimonials to the greatness of Ancient Egypt. Even further south, in the region known as Upper Egypt, there are hundreds of magnificent monuments and temples enhanced with hieroglyphic inscriptions attesting to the historical significance of that culture. Magically, the River Nile divides into two main branches near Cairo, the city which throughout history has had different names, languages, rulers, and most certainly, religions. The Damietta branch runs north-east and the Rosetta branch streams north-west. The rich verdant delta created between Damietta and Rosetta has always prevailed as a virtual paradise on earth. In contrast and far to the west of the Rosetta branch, lies the barren cruel Western Sahara which is known for its extreme and severe climate. There are many oasis in the Western Sahara which miraculously provide enough provisions for nomadic Bedouin tribes. Loyal and attached to their own, Bedouin are noted, among other things, for their generosity and success in commercial ventures.

Early on the fifth day of March 1811, dawn gently began to illuminate the sky and outshine the starry night of Egypt's Western Sahara. Warm southern breezes softly merged with the coolness of the passing night to announce an early beautiful Spring. Only the half moon shone brilliantly among the gradually fading stars, signalling the end of the first week of an Arabic lunar month. Unhurriedly, the moon would then progress into fullness over the next seven days. In the Arab world, a full moon signifies the middle of a lunar month and its brightness is used as a metaphor to describe a beautiful woman's face. Over the oasis, the moon shone through sturdy branches of numerous towering palm trees that rhythmically danced to the beat of the soft gentle breeze. In the vicinity, a Bedouin tribe slept peacefully in their multi-coloured tents. Despite its harshness, the desert is their home and the only place for them to be. Their camels, horses, sheep, and goats were safely guarded by the watchful eyes of several dogs. The ambiance was peaceful and calm, a model for harmony and tranquility in anticipation of a new day.

Suddenly, several barks pierced the pleasant transition from darkness to dawn. The yapping echoed throughout the encampment confirming a slow approaching mule. Yet, most inhabitants were not alarmed as they knew that such howls implied no danger. A few half-sleepy boys walked directly towards the oncoming animal wondering whether the rider was asleep, wounded, or both. They quietly gazed at each other uttering no words. An armed elderly tribesman cautiously shouted at them to stop while vigilantly heading towards the apparent intruder. Before he could get close enough, the unknown rider fell helplessly to the ground. With his sword pointed at the heart of the man, the tribesman apprehensively uncovered the stranger's face, moved away in surprise, and shouted to the boys, "May Allah be Praised! It's Zafaran *Bey*! Call on Salama and Sheik Abdullah to come immediately and bring a jug of water!"

In almost no time, Salama, chieftain of the tribe, and Sheik Abdullah, an elder, arrived at the scene. Salama was a little over six feet tall and in his early forties. He was a proud descendant of a legendary Bedouin tribe that had wandered Egypt's Western Sahara. Like many of the region's Bedouin, his tribe considered themselves free, belonging to no country and owing no loyalty to anyone, not even the Sultan. Despite his natural kindness, gentleness, and scrawny appearance, he could slaughter a camel with a single blow of his dagger.

They assisted Zafaran *Bey* off the ground and urged him to drink some water. His ragged clothes and most of his body were covered with sand and dust. He had a magnificently studded dagger at his waist and an unmistakably expensive sword by his side. His apparent weariness and exhaustion seemed to vanish as he saw Salama and Sheik Abdullah. With an inquisitive agonized look, he stared at the two men.

Salama volunteered, "Zafaran *Bey*! Your wife and children are safe. They are here in a tent with my wife." While kneeling next to the injured man, he then added, "Your father-in-law should now be on his way back from Cairo. With the help of some of my men, he should be able to bring more money and as many valuables as they can manage to carry."

Finally, Zafaran *Bey* smiled and with some difficulty adjusted his position. "I really don't know how to thank all of you for taking care of my family. May God bless you!"

"You're one of us, brother. Please, consider it a family duty," Sheik Abdullah replied.

"As you undoubtedly know, Egypt is no longer safe for you," Salama said cautiously and then added, "After you have recovered, you and your family may consider travelling to Syria. I know of a commercial caravan that will soon be on its way and, if necessary, I would gladly accompany you."

"I'm indebted to you all for my life and the life of my family. I don't know how to give thanks and I'm truly fortunate to be considered as one of you. May God Almighty reward you now and in the thereafter!" Zafaran *Bey* replied.

As the sun was about to rise on the eastern horizon, Salama and Sheik Abdullah assisted Zafaran *Bey* to a large tent at the western side of the encampment. They also helped him wash his body thoroughly before a medicine man examined his injuries. Following a few hours of treatment with animal and plant extracts, the medicine man looked at Salama and declared, "He is a strong man. Miraculously nothing seems serious. He should be able to walk and ride again in a couple of days provided that he rests, drinks a lot of goat milk, and eats camel meat."

Salama assured the medicine man that all his instructions and guidance would be followed and politely walked him out of the tent. Meanwhile, Salwa, Zafaran *Bey*'s wife entered from an adjoining compartment with their children. Heartbroken and with tearful eyes, the family approached the bed. Zafaran *Bey* smiled at them reassuringly and whispered, "Just give me a couple of days and I will be able to carry all of you with one hand."

The children were happy and relieved. They laughed and began kissing their father tenderly. It was a joyful family reunion. A few moments later, a heavy elderly woman entered and gently led the children to another compartment leaving the happy couple alone. As they moved reluctantly towards the entrance, the children complied and went along while looking back at their parents.

"Frankly, my love, it was a miracle! I still don't believe what has happened or that I'm here with you and the children," declared a mystified Zafaran *Bey*. He then continued, "There is no way to describe the horror I went through. It was like hell had fallen onto earth!"

Salwa touched and kissed him affectionately and offered, "My love, now that you're here with us, we're all safe. Thanks to Allah that we're away from Cairo and its wretchedness. Have you had any trouble on your way?"

"No! I had none whatsoever, thanks to Allah. I was disguised as a poor Bedouin and no one bothered me on the way here."

Salwa inquired, "Then, how did you receive these injuries?"

"I'll tell you all about it later. How was your trip from Cairo?"

"It was almost perfect. The children were happy and Salama's men followed us from a distance. We have been treated here like family."

"And your father! Is he all right?"

"He was fine until he heard the dreadful news from Cairo. He decided to return to bring more money and other valuable items."

"I'm sure he'll be happy to see me."

"I was told that Damascus would be safer for us. Do you think so?"

With some difficulty, Zafaran *Bey* took a deep breath and then with a bizarre gesture, asked himself aloud, "How the devil can one man commit such ghoulish atrocities?" The horrors of the last few days had triggered anger and rage in his heart. Irrationally, he considered revenge; however, realistically he was content to be alive. A wave of depression beset him and his senses momentarily froze while doubts affected his state of mind. He then realized that his wife had just asked him a question. He looked into her eyes and said gravely, "You know how much I love this country but as long as that tyrant Mohammed Ali is in control, we have no choice but to leave quietly for Damascus."

"Yes, my love, and my father will accompany us wherever we go."

Zafaran *Bey* anxiously inquired, "And when is our baby due?"

"It could possibly be in a few days."

"I know we're quite safe here, God bless our friends! Yet, we'll prepare for departure anyway."

"My love, whatever you decide. The children missed you very much and now they're happy that you're here."

The happy couple embraced one another passionately as they hoped for a new future in Damascus.

1

While promising to liberate Egyptians from the tyrant Mamelukes and also claiming to be a Muslim and a friend of the Ottoman Sultan, Napoleon Bonaparte ruthlessly invaded Egypt in 1798 leading the first European army to venture into that region since the crusaders. Only a month after a jubilant victory in Cairo, his fleet was totally destroyed by the English on the shores of the Mediterranean. Unexpectedly, and nearly a year later, Napoleon abandoned his stranded army and fled Egypt back to France. Undoubtedly, his departure constituted a shocking blow to everyone particularly General Klébre who had to assume command of a futile mission. In late 1801, a settlement had been reached through English mediation between the Ottoman Empire and France. Accordingly, French troops, under the command of General Menou, would ultimately capitulate and withdraw from Egypt with full military honours. Egypt would then return to its former invader and occupier, the Ottoman Empire.

The Ottoman Empire, despite its military might and regardless of the apparent political victory at the time, had difficulties controlling its vast territories. Regaining Egypt from the French added another burden to its already weakening structure. Moreover, the French departure created an opportunity for a serious power struggle between the Ottomans, the present occupier, and their old local rivals, the Mamelukes.

The Mamelukes considered themselves the legitimate owners and rightful rulers of Egypt. As they recognized the weakening of the Ottomans, they saw the possibility of their return to power. From mostly East-European slave origin dating back to Saladin's time, the Mamelukes leaders were known as the Egyptian *Emirs* and had always been a formidable military power. They also claimed and controlled most of Egypt's agricultural land, the source of endless wealth and prosperity. In addition, the Mamelukes imposed enormous taxes on common Egyptians, allowing themselves a lavish and luxurious lifestyle. Amazingly, throughout their history, they were known to be extremely brave and fearless of death with a complete and incomprehensible disconnection from reality. They were also famous for their extravagantly decorated weapons, exceptionally elegant clothes, and marvellously groomed Arabian horses. Their appreciation for jewellery, art, and architecture were unsurpassed. The fantastic lifestyle of the Mamelukes was suddenly shattered by the Ottoman's invasion of Egypt. Due to the enormous Mameluke population which spread throughout the country, the conquering Ottoman Turks endured their presence but kept a watchful eye over their leaders.

Cairo, the city of over a thousand minarets, was in the process of welcoming a new sunrise. While the sun spread its warmth over each and every street and narrow lane, merchants, shopkeepers, artisans, water carriers, beggars, musicians, and dancers looked forward to a new fruitful day. As everything else, commerce in Cairo was different. Each and every commodity had its own marketplace at distinct quarters of the city. Vegetables, fruits, clothes, gold, jewels, livestock, seeds, slaves, tobacco, perfumes, and furniture each had a separate souk.

Dust rose in one direction following the horses ridden by units of Ottoman soldiers while silt in the opposite direction swirled after the horses ridden by groups of Mamelukes. Though the French had long been out of the country, an everlasting European touch still lingered over the city. Restaurants and coffee shops remained there in certain districts. Many women, mostly foreigners, adopted styles of clothing that resembled European ones. In general terms, the outlook of Cairo had somehow altered a little. Although most Cairenes had considered the French as infidels, later they realized that they were at least honest compared with the Ottoman occupiers.

*****

Earlier than his usual time, Shookry the barber was about to start his daily work at a recently acquired location near a mosque in Cairo. His two neighbours, one on each side, were already at work shaving the heads of young clients. Disappointed not to be the first to arrive, Shookry was surprised to see them already at work. He greeted them politely, took three sheep-skin mats out of his huge sack, and unrolled them carefully on the dusty ground. To his surprise, as he was about to erect the sun shed and take his blades and other tools out of a leather case, a seemingly well-to-do middle-aged client, expecting to be served, approached and sat comfortably on the mat.

"Welcome, and a fine blessed morning to you, *Emir*!" Shookry started cheerfully then continued, "What may I do for you? May I order coffee now or later and would you allow me to place your headgear next to you over here?"

"Give me a head shave and slightly trim my beard. No thanks, no coffee," replied the client in an agitated tone. He then inquired, "You took Sheik Haleem's spot, didn't you?"

Shookry noticed the agitation and found the question disturbing yet he politely decided to elevate his client's title from *Emir* to *Pasha*. "Yes, Pasha, May God prolong your life! Sheik

Haleem has recently passed away. May God Almighty have mercy on his soul! Let's all recite the *Fateha*, the opening verse of the Holy Koran, on his soul."

The two men, as well as others who were listening, moved their lips in silence reciting the *Fateha*. After a few moments of silence, the client proclaimed in a less agitated tone, "Sheik Haleem, May God have mercy on his soul, was a good man, indeed!"

Shookry nodded several times in agreement while sharpening his blade on a long strap of black leather. He then poured an oily liquid and gently rubbed it evenly over the man's pate. A while later, he carefully began to shave his client's bare head while listening to a faint sound of music coming from the nearby bustling market. Unable to control himself, Shookry began humming along with the music.

While feeling the sharp blade move smoothly over his skin, the client asked quietly, "Have you taken charge of Sheik Haleem's other affairs as well?"

Shookry asked in surprise, "What other affairs, Pasha?"

"Well, like performing circumcision and shaving the pubic hair of newlywed men."

"Certainly, Pasha, and I've had many years of practice," Shookry proudly answered.

"Well, the reason I'm asking is that my son will soon be due for circumcision."

Shookry's eyes gleamed with anticipation and he knew he could not elevate the title he had superficially bestowed upon his new client to Sultan because that title is reserved for the leader of an Empire and not just for a rich man.

"Pasha, May God Almighty protect and raise your son in prosperity and contentment! It would be my greatest honour to perform, with the highest precision, the circumcision of your beloved son." He then curiously inquired, "When Pasha ... when ... where?"

Shookry knew that performing circumcision for a rich family could mean quite a lot of rewards for him. He might then buy his wife and children some good food, new clothes, and badly needed household items as well. Shookry was thrilled yet realized that the least he could do was to suppress his excitement until he had actually been hired for the job. He quietly washed and dried the shaving blade, tucked it carefully into his leather bag, and retrieved a pair of scissors and a wooden comb. While having difficulties in suppressing his emotions, he began trimming his client's beard.

After a moment of silence, his client finally continued, "God willing! This coming Friday, shortly following the prayers is the time. Family, friends, and the whole neighbourhood already know that. I've asked Sheik Haleem, God Bless his soul, at least a month ago."

Shookry kept calm while prolonging the beard-trimming process. He asked, "And where is your palace, Pasha?"

"Behind El-Shafee Mosque, the third palace to the right. You only need to mention my name, *Emir* Moustafa El-Gandour, and thousands of people will point at my palace. Come a little earlier so that all goes on time."

The beard-trimming continued at its normal pace and was accompanied by a spontaneous smile on Shookry's face. He could not resist imagining himself dressed in his white well-preserved *galabeya*, a long shirt-like garment, carrying his dark brown leather bag, and respectfully being greeted by many dignitaries and guests at *Emir* Moustafa El-Gandour's palace. Shookry responded without hesitation, "God willing! I'll certainly arrive as early as possible."

As Shookry was dusting hair off *Emir* El-Gandour's shoulders with a horsetail brush, a new client arrived and sat quietly on a mat to the left. While putting his client's headgear back on his head, Shookry asked quietly, "Could I bring my nine-year old son, Mohsen, as helper? This morning he is at the *kuttab* (school) and, with your permission, he would gain some experience for his future profession."

Emir Moustafa El-Gandour examined the new client waiting on the fur mat. He then discreetly slipped a small purse full of coins in Shookry's hand.

"This is just a little thing for now and, by the way, if you want, you can bring your whole neighbourhood to attend the celebration."

"Thank you, Pasha. May God bless and prolong your life, Pasha! May God bless and protect all your children and grandchildren!"

Shookry courteously bowed several times and kept repeating his remarks and thanks until *Emir* Moustafa El-Gandour vanished into the crowd.

While trying hard to somehow suppress the smile on his face and appear natural, Shookry absentmindedly invited his next client to approach and be seated. As he began shaving him, he noticed his son, Mohsen, arriving from the *kuttab*.

"You seem to have struck a good deal today," said his fellow barber on the right.

"Moustafa El-Gandour usually shows up once a year but now that he has lately become an *Emir,* we might never see him again," exclaimed his fellow barber on the left.

"You two, just keep your evil eyes off me. Well, May God protect me from your wickedness and keep the demons only on your side, not mine," Shookry responded jokingly. Their loud laughter drew the attention of some passers-by.

Mohsen greeted his father and the others, "May peace be upon you all!" He then took a swatter and began chasing flies from around his father's new client.

Shookry checked with his client, "Welcome master Awaad. Would you like a coffee or anything else?"

Awaad replied, "No, thanks. Not now. Was that *Emir* Moustafa El-Gandour who has just left?"

"Yes! He has hired me to perform circumcision on his son next week."

Another customer came and waited to be served. As a result, Shookry hurriedly shaved Awaad's head and took less than one hour to complete the job. Awaad then paid and bid him goodbye.

At the end of his working day, Shookry and his son collected their equipment, rolled it carefully, and left. On their way home, Shookry bought bread, fruit, and a lot of dried dates. He also purchased a nicely decorated headscarf and a pair of earrings for his wife. He treated his son to a sweet sherbet drink and also generously donated bread to many of the beggars he encountered. At the mosque, they performed the fifth and last prayer of the day. In addition, Shookry told his son that he would perform an extra prayer to thank God for today's generous offer. When they were about to leave the mosque, Shookry heard a familiar voice.

"Why don't we now have coffee in that establishment across the street?"

"What a nice surprise, master Awaad. I certainly would love to but, unfortunately, we have to go now. We have guests awaiting us at home," Shookry responded.

"Would it be possible tomorrow then at the same time?" Awaad persisted.

"Yes, of course! I'll be happy to have coffee with you over there tomorrow."

"I'll be waiting for you!"

2

Almost a year earlier, Moustafa El-Gandour, formerly a Mameluke, had become an *Emir*. Due to his loyalty, leadership qualities, and extraordinary courage, he earned his freedom and title from his master. As *Emir* he would then be entitled to many privileges including tax collection from certain districts and, most importantly, he could also purchase foreign Mameluke boys for training to become his own loyal protectors and warriors. In no time, *Emir* Moustafa El-Gandour knew exactly how to establish his position among the many other *Emirs* and even surpass some of them in both power and prestige. Though he already had a few hundred cavalry at his service and many other men were undergoing rigorous training, his ambitions dictated the necessity of attaining more. In addition to his two magnificent palaces in Cairo, he also owned several farms in the most fertile regions of the Nile's delta. Furthermore, and to confirm his religious devotion, he had recently built a magnificent mosque in central Cairo with a captivating tall minaret.

While leisurely and proudly riding his Arabian horse towards his palace, *Emir* El-Gandour could still feel the barber's blade over his head. On several occasions, he removed his head cover and felt for blood but there was none. He had never forgotten his first head shaving experience which had been administered by a cruel barber who worked for Shatabgy, the slave trader. Old images of himself and a few dozen slave boys screaming throughout that torturous exercise flashed through his mind. What sometimes troubled *Emir* El-Gandour was the fact that he could neither remember his parents nor his place of origin. Another predicament that truly haunted him was whether he had been sold by his parents or simply kidnapped from them by Shatabgy. Sadly, the only recollection from his childhood was a blurred memory of a wooden cabin and high trees surrounded by strange looking mountains with white tops. Despite the vague and troublesome aspects of such elusive memories, he tended to believe and disbelieve them all at the same time. Now that he was in his mid thirties and a proud father, he should not bother himself with the past.

His disturbing thoughts vanished from his mind as he approached his palace. Pride and satisfaction filled his heart and a sense of personal greatness overtook him. The palace, which he had purchased from a Turkish officer whose term had ended in Cairo, was a true marvel of architecture. *Emir* El-Gandour reconstructed had and expanded the palace by hiring the best builders and artisans he could find in the city. His vast gardens were always well-groomed and resplendent with fruit trees.

On arrival, *Emir* El-Gandour was courteously received by two of his own Mamelukes. A servant immediately took care of the horse and bowed as *Emir* El-Gandour walked towards the magnificently carved door. A Mameluke politely informed him that Zafaran *Bey* had requested an audience with him regarding an urgent matter upon which *Emir* El-Gandour ordered, "Send a messenger to inform Zafaran *Bey* that he may come anytime he pleases." He then entered his *dewan* (office) where a few other Mamelukes were assisting an accountant and a scribe in their work. They all attempted to stand up as a sign of respect yet *Emir* El-Gandour casually motioned to them to sit and continue. He also informed one of his assistants that he would be in his guestroom awaiting Zafaran *Bey*.

A water-pipe crowned with glowing charcoal diffused the unique aroma of an expensive Turkish tobacco. It was carefully placed by a servant on a shiny copper tray in front of *Emir* El-Gandour who sought comfort on a soft pillow. The floor of the grand guestroom was covered with a collection of expensive Persian carpets. Countless pillows of different sizes and styles were scattered decoratively around the perimeter. Low tables of fine wood carried shimmering trays heavily-laden with all sorts of fruit and other delicacies. A large window overlooked a magnificent garden allowing the pleasant scent of jasmine and roses to fill the air. When the first drag of Turkish smoke entered *Emir* El-Gandour's enormous lungs, he immediately realized that the persistent itchiness on his shaven head had disappeared. His earlier thoughts about his childhood mysteriously vanished and he could sense that his power and prominence not only embraced his palace but also the entire city of Cairo. Though unrealistic, he sometimes thought that he could take over and rule the entire country. He strongly believed that Egypt belonged to his own breed of the Mamelukes and that the Ottoman Turks had neither the right nor the military power to sustain an Ottoman stronghold. He regarded them as opportunistic vampires who ruthlessly sucked the blood of any nation they conquered. Despite palpable complications, he had always advocated unity among the Mamelukes as the only way to defeat and expel the Ottoman Turks from Egypt. While sitting, one of his Mamelukes politely walked in and announced the arrival of Zafaran *Bey*. *Emir* El-Gandour billowed clouds of smoke and curiously observed them dispersing into the air. He then stood up as Zafaran *Bey* approached him.

"Welcome, my dear friend," *Emir* El-Gandour embraced and warmly greeted his guest in a brotherly fashion. He then pointed to a huge cushion next to his and invited Zafaran *Bey* to take a seat. A well-dressed servant brought a second water-pipe while another began serving coffee. The two men continued to exchange niceties and pleasant conversation while the aroma of fresh coffee combined with tobacco smoke filled the hall blending with the fresh breeze coming through the large window.

"It seems certain, according to my informants, that Mohammed Ali will soon invite us all to celebrate his son's departure to Arabia," Zafaran *Bey* said with a serious gesture.

"Should that be a reason to worry?"

"Well, besides the fact that he hates us, I find such an invitation to be odd and disturbing," replied Zafaran *Bey*.

"I know what you mean. Mohammed Ali is a man not to be trusted! Surprisingly, he has been the governor now for several years. That's well beyond any normal term. It's quite strange that the Sultan never replaced him by sending another Pasha from Constantinople, as he usually does!"

Zafaran *Bey* waited a little and then replied, "Strangely enough, there have been several popular support groups in favour of Mohammed Ali to remain as Governor. He has unprecedented support from religious leaders, trade guilds, and many notable merchants. More surprising is the exceptional enthusiasm for him among the average populace."

"What? People's enthusiasm! What has that to do with an appointed governor? That is certainly new to me!"

Zafaran *Bey* waited, puffed out a few clouds of smoke, and then replied, "The people of Cairo seem happy with Mohammed Ali's appointment. That is definitely why his term as governor has well exceeded the usual two years. Whatever the argument may be, Mohammed Ali is the Pasha of Egypt."

"Way back, when he was an officer, I still recall the mystery surrounding the death of his commander. Or, should I say the assassination of his troop leader. Isn't it strange that he became the commander right after? Are you surprised that now he is the Pasha of Egypt? All seems like one deliberate scheme after another by a cunning and wicked fox, don't you think?"

Zafaran *Bey* stood, walked towards a window, then said, "The present chaos, disarray, and the economic situation does not really tempt anyone to be a governor, so why would he?"

"I really don't know the answer to that one. But, one thing is certain, he hates us. He would pay any price to see us all dead. Therefore, my friend, I'll arrange for a meeting to discuss and debate that proposed invitation whenever we get it."

"Whatever Mohammed Ali may do, we must unite and be vigilant about each and every move he makes. Even if that move seems to be at our advantage, it could also be a carefully planned entrapment. One way or another, he's not to be trusted. Many actions by him and his soldiers have clearly proven that," responded Zafaran *Bey*.

Emir El-Gandour waited, and then said, "Regarding another subject, a shipment of weapons and ammunition, which I have ordered along with other *Emirs*, has arrived by sea at a location near Alexandria. It's now being transported by a friendly Bedouin tribe to Cairo through the western desert. The quality is high and the prices are fair. If you care to acquire some for your men, let me know soon."

"Although I've recently purchased a large amount of weaponry and ammunition, I would certainly be interested. Inform me when it arrives."

"I sure will! It's just a matter of days. Now, on another matter, and this is definitely between the two of us. I'm exploring a plan to have an informant in Mohammed Ali's organization. If I succeed, you'll be the first to know," said *Emir* El-Gandour in a whispering tone.

"That sounds great. But as a friend, let me warn you since that could be extremely dangerous. That informant of yours might be an informant of yet another informant."

"I know, but it's a risk that may prove worth taking."

After nearly an hour of friendly conversation, Zafaran *Bey* took his leave. Later, he was lovingly received by his beautiful wife and children.

3

Smoking tobacco and coffee-drinking were, and still are, some of the unadorned pleasures most Egyptians enjoy specially when socializing. Tobacco drenched in molasses, not to mention its enrichment with other fruit flavours, provides a delightful indulgence for smokers. Tobacco lovers, rich or poor, enjoy inhaling smoke from water-pipes that significantly differ in material, design, craftsmanship, quality and, of course, prices. The most primitive water-pipe is known as *goza* which is the Arabic word for a coconut. It is usually made up of three basic parts. The first is a small simple clay holder for tobacco and charcoal. The second is a hollow coconut shell to hold some water for smoke filtration and finally, the third is a bamboo pipe to serve as a mouthpiece. The three parts are cleverly attached together so that, when a user sucks air through the mouthpiece, charcoal kindles the tobacco, allowing its smoke to be filtered through water before reaching the lungs.

The hall was dimly lit by a few oil lamps which hung on dirty grayish walls. The patrons, mostly common workingmen, occupied mainly the perimeter and sat in somewhat comfortable positions on rags, goat-skin mats or on the bare dusty floor. The large front door was widely open allowing a view of the bustling street, and also to lure new clients into the establishment. Those inside held in their hands cheap primitive water-pipes of the *goza* type. They produced ample clouds of heavy smoke contributing even more to the murkiness of the hall. Despite the number of regulars, the hall was relatively quiet even though occasional loud laughter could be heard at one time or another. Contrary to the custom in other similar places, the host would collect money before service was rendered. Through an opening at the far end, a woman and a young girl tended to an archaic brick-oven loaded with glowing charcoal ready to be served. Occasionally, when a beggar, usually blind, crippled or both, somehow managed to get in, he would politely be asked to leave. In some rare instances, such intruders might get a tiny coin or otherwise they were simply ignored. Street vendors were certainly a different horde altogether. They knew all the rules of this establishment. They might yell, scream or even blow their horns outside, but they could not set foot inside unless invited by a client. Yet, strangely enough, storytellers, singers, and musicians, particularly when accompanied by young female dancers, were usually granted permission to enter. Not only were they allowed a short stay, but were also rewarded by a *goza* on the house as well.

*****

Though it was early in the evening and fairly clear, Shookry, the barber, had difficulty seeing when he entered the smoky dimly-lit hall. He tried to scrutinize all the faces that gawked at him but he could not recognize his client, Awaad. He attempted a second round of inspection but to no avail. Abruptly, a disturbing voice almost pierced his left ear.

The host asked him in a rough agitated voice, "What will it be? Goza, coffee, or both?"

Shookry turned around in surprise to respond to the voice and noticed a huge man with a puffed-up face and exceptionally large round eyes. He hesitated while his mind quickly raced and condemned the idea of agreeing to meet with Awaad and have a coffee with him. He then gathered his courage and said in a steady voice, "I'm looking for master Awaad. He's supposed to be waiting for me here."

Suddenly, the host's face broke into a faint smile and his tone became less coarse than earlier.

"Master Awaad was here a while ago. He'll be back shortly. Please, sit on that mat over there. I'll send you a *goza* and coffee."

Without having to pay in advance, Shookry sipped his coffee and added smoke to the already dense air. As his vision gradually grew accustomed to the darkness, most faces around him were fairly visible. The patrons he observed were not the kind of clients he would want to see at his barber-stand. At the same time, he also wondered about Awaad's choice of this meeting place. A little later, he realized that people paid before being served and asked himself why he had been exempted, at least for now. As the smoke streamed out of his nostrils, he again thought of Awaad, who came regularly to his barber-stand as a client. Oddly enough, they had become acquaintances of a sort: *Who is he anyway? What does he do for a living? Why meet at this place?* These puzzling questions raced through his head, making his presence in the hall uncomfortable. He seriously debated the idea of leaving quietly. Adding to his perplexity, a boy came and handed him a freshly prepared *goza* while taking away the one he had just finished smoking. He somehow tried to reassure himself: *Well! It isn't really as bad as it seemed to be.* Smoke began to spread above his head from the newly-served *goza* while he tried to convince himself that Awaad was just an ordinary man and that there was, in fact, nothing unusual about the hall in which he sat. From time to time, he gazed at the patrons around him and then turned his attention to the street through the wide door frame on his right. All of a sudden, the unmistakably burly figure of Awaad appeared in the center of the hall. Radiating power and alertness, Awaad walked towards Shookry with open arms and the two men embraced.

"I hope you didn't wait for long," Awaad uttered, "I just remembered something important that I had to do."

"No, no. It's quite all right. I just came in a short while ago myself."

Before Shookry could sit back on the mat, the newly-served *goza* had been replaced by yet another and a fresh cup of coffee was placed next to it. Puzzled, Shookry quietly sipped his coffee and puffed a few more clouds of smoke.

"Are you a regular client of this place?" asked Shookry.

"Yes, I'm a regular and I also own the place," Awaad answered laughingly. "I know it's not one of my best places, but I always liked the location."

"You mean you own other places as well?"

"A few here, a few there. To be exact, eight altogether."

"With seven other establishments even better than this one, then you're a rich man, Awaad. May God bless all your possessions and enrich you even more!"

"Well, thank you. You may think it's simple to run such an operation but let me assure you, my friend, that it isn't as easy as many may think. The way things are now, especially after the French had left, you could get yourself killed in the process. No matter how much money you've got, if you're not a Mameluke or Ottoman Turk, you're nothing! "

Mystified, Shookry wondered why he had come to meet someone like Awaad who seemed to be dissatisfied with all he had. He wondered again while finishing his coffee: *What seems to be his problem if he has as many establishments generating money as he claims? And why am I here listening to all this?* He carefully put his cup on the metal tray and was about to respond.

"But we deserve better, much better than that, my dear friend. Don't you think so?" Awaad said calmly.

"Yes, of course! How can we do that?" Shookry asked, yet he really did not care much about the answer.

"With iron and fire, my friend, iron and fire. Of course, they're militarily trained, possess weapons, horses, and most of all, each group bands tightly together when in danger, but we're smarter, much smarter than they may think. Our brain, my friend, is the iron and fire I'm talking about. Think, think clearly, then you'll get what I really mean."

Shookry nodded in agreement as if, somehow, he had finally seen the light from afar. He absent-mindedly dragged an enormous amount of smoke into his lungs and released it in a slow and methodical manner.

"Would you help me out?" Awaad asked.

"Me, help you! You know that I'm only a simple barber. How can I possibly help?"

Awaad pulled a tiny sack out of his pocket and pushed it into Shookry's hand.

"Here is your reward in advance, if you agree. Open it carefully and have a look. There'll certainly be more if all goes well."

"Five coins in gold! That could possibly be more than all my earnings in many months."

In disbelief, Shookry held the tiny sack tightly in his hand.

"What sort of help do you expect in return for such a treasure? Kill someone?"

"Simple! Very simple! Just let me accompany you to the circumcision of *Emir* Moustafa El-Gandour's son. That is all and nothing else."

"What? What do you mean?" asked Shookry.

"All you have to do is to allow me to walk with you into *Emir* Moustafa El-Gandour's palace. I'll be disguised as an elderly assistant and will even carry your bag for you. I'll look so old and unimportant that no one will ever notice me."

With the tiny purse held firmly in his fist, Shookry was doubtful and suspicious.

"But I already asked for my son to be my assistant and *Emir* El-Gandour agreed. Seems too late for my help."

"Look! Your son may still go with you as a guest and companion. Only if they ask you about me, though I doubt they will, then you may introduce me as your older experienced helper. Once I'm inside the palace, my dear friend, neither you nor anybody else will see or even remember me again. Once there, you do what you have to do, and then leave with your son."

After a moment of silence, Awaad reassured him by offering a second tiny sack of gold.

"Here is another purse! Finish your *goza*, take the gold home and think about it. Tomorrow, at the same time, I'll be right here to meet you. You may then decide to help me or return all the gold."

"For someone like me, it all sounds very strange. All I can say now is that whatever my decision may possibly be; I'll let you know about it tomorrow."

With two small purses each containing five golden coins, Shookry went home confused and baffled about an offer he could not simply rebuff. The rewards were too good to ignore considering that practically he was not expected to do a thing in return. In fact, a good deal of money was offered for such a simple request. He would possess enough gold to grant him and his family a good and comfortable life for a long time. A piece of land out in the country to live on would be an attractive option. Many other entrepreneurial ideas dazzled his mind and the fact that he carried the gold on him increased his fantastic reveries. Flying like a bird, walking safely over the waters of the Nile, or even extinguishing blazing flames with a touch of one hand were only a few of the amazing powers he imagined he had. With a special dignity and pride, he walked and felt superior to all those around him. Suddenly, he realized that his left hand was still carrying the barber's bag. Shookry was about to dump the sack with all his strength when he recognized that he must still remain a barber until he had performed the circumcision on *Emir* Moustafa El-Gandour's son and received the other golden coins from Awaad. From a stand near his home, he bought bread and fruit and walked proudly with his hands full.

Once inside his home, his mother-in-law gave him the usual look, his father-in-law was praying and Hooda, Shookry's wife, tended a huge pot of food on a primitive clay stove while holding their baby daughter. The heat and smoke emitted from the burning wood could be sensed everywhere inside the hall and the two small rooms. He dropped his work bag in a corner near the door and placed the fruit next to his wife. Shookry then went into the bedroom and threw himself over the large bed-mat on the floor. Hooda entered and placed the baby on another carpet next to theirs and inquired, "What's the matter? How did it go with that client of yours, Awaad? Did you go and have coffee with him?"

"Yes! I had coffee with him at his own establishment. Imagine! He actually owns a few others as well."

"Well, he must be a rich man, then."

The baby started to cry. Shookry picked her up, kissed her, and handed her to Hooda who immediately began to breastfeed the infant. Shookry was not sure whether or not to reveal the issue of gold to his wife at this moment or keep it to himself. From past experiences, he realized that his mother-in-law could be listening and he would have to endure her unwanted ideas and opinions. He observed his wife and the baby calmly and decided to wait. He finally asked, "Where is Mohsen?"

"He is still playing with other children in the alley. He should be back soon for supper. Earlier he had been telling everyone how happy he was to join you at the circumcision celebration."

"The food is ready and I'll be serving! Someone should call the boy in," announced the mother-in-law in a rough and agitated voice.

Shookry took the sleepy baby and put her back on the mat. He left the room followed by his wife and saw the huge plate of freshly-cooked meat and vegetables in the center of the low table. He was about to go and call on Mohsen when the exhausted youngster entered through the main door. The family sat around the large platter to enjoy their last meal of the day.

Later in their bedroom, when Shookry was certain that his son was asleep, he retrieved a golden coin from one of the two small purses he had in his pocket. The coin magically sparkled in the dim light of the tiny oil-lamp. When Hooda noticed it, she almost shrieked as Shookry handed it to her. Carefully, she held the tiny treasure with her delicate fingers as a bright smile formed instantaneously on her beautiful face. Surprised, she gazed at her husband inquisitively and asked, "How did you get it? Did you find it?"

"I have nine more just like it with me here!"

Astonished, Hooda replied excitedly, "What? Nine more are here with you. Show me! Show me!"

With somewhat shaky hands, Shookry spread the contents of both tiny purses over the bed. As nine golden coins tinkled, Hooda's face became brighter and brighter. Suddenly, a stream of unstoppable tears rolled down her cheeks. For a while Hooda and Shookry clutched tightly to each other in a fervent embrace. They frantically began kissing one another and made love on top of the glittering metal. Overwhelmed with ecstasy and excitement, they rolled over the gold as their bodies undulated until pleasurable spasms overtook them in that blissful moment of oneness. They fell back exhausted with the metal pieces adhering to their bodies.

Hours later, Shookry and Hooda searched the floor for each single coin and counted them one by one then returned them to the purses so that the ten coins were secured. Shookry placed the purses under his pillow and then began relating to Hooda in a sleepy and relaxed manner his meeting with Awaad. At the end of his story, he stressed the fact that Awaad would give him ten more coins after taking him to the palace where the circumcision was to take place.

"Although the rewards are generous, somehow I feel uneasy about his strange request to enter the palace. I hope there will be no danger to you and neither to our son!" Hooda uttered worriedly.

"I see no danger at all. Once I get him inside, he'll vanish and disappear. That's what he has said and I believe him."

"Well, my love, what's next then?"

"I have to see him again tomorrow and let him know whether I accept the deal or return the coins."

"And have you decided yet?"

"To tell you the truth, my mind wasn't made up until we both rolled over those damn coins and had such pleasure."

"And!"

"I'll accept Awaad's proposition. It's for all of us."

4

Though circumcision is a sober and serious undertaking, it also calls for cheerfulness and celebration among families, friends, and neighbours. Usually performed by a barber on boys between the age of three and six, circumcision is considered to be a way of purifying the body in the Islamic tradition. It is celebrated as a day of merriment among average families and may even extend for a few days by the well-to-do. Sweetmeats, flavoured sherbet drinks, and food of all kinds are expected to be served and to be enjoyed by all. In addition to the actual festivity inside the home or palace, generosity and goodwill inspire rich families to display a special buffet for all in the neighbourhood and passers-by. Music, chants, and recitation of the Holy Koran at times become also part of the celebration. Surprisingly, many Cairo beggars have ways of knowing where and when such feasts may be organized by rich families so that they may enjoy their fair share of scrumptious delicacies as well.

After the Friday prayers, *Emir* Moustafa El-Gandour and many of his family and friends gathered in front of the mosque. Shookry the barber, his son and, of course, disguised Awaad were surprised to see the jubilant crowd waiting outside the mosque. Close-by, they saw the perplexed youngster who was about to be circumcised. As customs dictated, the boy was dressed in a long white shirt, donned a white cap on his head, and was sitting on the saddle in reverse position with his head facing the rear of a well-decorated horse. A family member helped secure the boy while a servant held the horse's harness and kept the animal under control. A group of musicians began to signal the start of the procession. Shookry, his son, and Awaad followed *Emir* Moustafa El-Gandour and all the others as they walked enthusiastically behind the garlanded horse. At the far end of the procession, a group of veiled women rejoiced by singing and chanting in a dignified and controlled manner.

As Awaad walked like an old man in his white caftan, Shookry carefully whispered into his son's ear, "I've never before circumcised a horse rider. If one of my clients ever had a ride, it was on a donkey."

His son asked, "I've never seen such decorations and so many flowers on one horse. Where do they get all that?"

"Son, money can get you anything!'

"Where do they live, father?"

"In a palace not far from here. After we do the job, I hope you'll have enough appetite to eat for a whole week. There'll be enough food to fill a pyramid or block the Nile."

Mohsen asked, "Do they always eat like that?"

"Probably they do. Remember, this is a special occasion as they tend to show off and overdo things."

During the procession to the palace, Awaad walked closely behind Shookry holding the barber's bag and lowering his head. He walked heavily, assuming difficulty in keeping pace with the parade. Suddenly a convoy of twenty Ottoman soldiers from an Albanian unit appeared in the opposite direction heading towards the joyful procession. The Albanians seemed to be in a hurry and their officer showed a grimace of discontent when he saw the joyful procession coming towards them. He shouted in a condescending tone and ordered the crowd in front of him to disperse immediately and clear the way. Yet, when he noticed that there were Mamelukes among the crowd including *Emir* Moustafa El-Gandour, his tone changed. Everything came to a halt on both sides.

"Let me take care of this," Zafaran *Bey* said.

He then walked directly to the Albanian officer, who was still mounted on his horse, and exchanged some formal greetings.

"We thought that you were about to join us in celebrating the circumcision of *Emir* Moustafa El-Gandour's son. But since you and your men seem to be in a hurry, we shall provide you with a passage if you allow us enough time to do it in an orderly fashion."

Despite his contempt for the Mamelukes, the Albanian officer dismounted his horse and motioned to his soldiers to do the same. They quietly walked through the crowd heading towards their destination. Once they were at a distance, the procession joyfully came to life again with music resounding even louder than before.

When they finally reached the palace, another crowd awaited them at the gate with more music and cold sherbet drinks. An elderly relative approached the horse and helped the young boy dismount. He then placed a red scarf on the boy's shoulders. Shookry and his son followed the elderly man who led the boy into the palace along with male relatives and friends. Meanwhile, Awaad remained as close as possible to Shookry until they reached the main hall inside the palace.

Sure enough, no one, including the guards, suspected or even paid any attention to Awaad who swiftly vanished into a long side corridor with large doors on both sides. He then carefully opened the third door to his right and quietly slipped in. He stood motionless by a wall observing each and every part of the room. Only when he was convinced that he was alone, did he begin to walk and examine the walls and anything that hung on them. Represented were the most unusual decorations: swords, protective shields, helmets, and even saddles used by cavalry. After an extensive examination of each item that he had seen, nothing resembled what he had been anticipating. Indisputably, he was in the room he sought yet nothing on the walls pointed to what he was searching for. Doubts and suspicions about his informants began to haunt him. He then realized that either he must immediately retreat or take a chance and try another room.

As he was about to reach for the door, his eyes spotted three decorative swords hanging on the main wall. Though they seemed identical and ordinary, the one on the left appeared slightly out of alignment with the other two and was placed somewhat lower. He stared at the three swords while mentally calculating the time still available to him in case he needed to check another room. Instinctively, he rushed back to the swords and began to examine them. Nothing seemed out of the ordinary until he attempted to remove the third one on the left. He discovered that this sword, unlike the other two, was not only attached to the wall but was actually part of it. Baffled and confused, Awaad marvelled at the artwork in front of him while touching the handle in admiration. Surprisingly, the sword handle swung a little forward. Impulsively, Awaad pulled it further down. Simultaneously, the entire wall moved almost thirty degrees inward creating an opening at its far end. Awaad's body froze.

For a while, his hand remained suspended in the air. Trying to control himself, he lit a candle from a nearby tray, and slowly walked towards the opening that allowed only one person through. Abruptly, he stopped and gazed back at the sword handle and wondered if it were a trap. Carefully placing the candle on a small table, he returned his attention to the sword and lifted the handle upright to its original position. Sure enough, the opening gradually vanished as the wall joined with the other creating a seamless perfect corner again. A smile appeared on Awaad's face as he observed with amazement the wall opening a second time. Holding the candle, he walked carefully through the narrow opening. The space resembled a stockroom heavily packed with gold and fabulous jewellery. Awaad walked in disbelief through a tiny area between two huge loaded shelves. He suddenly remembered the many storytellers, who recounted the tale of *Ali-Baba and the Forty Thieves*, at his establishments. He almost laughed aloud as he appreciated that he was, at the moment, the only Ali-Baba. As he spotted the item he had sought, he accepted the painful fact that he could not possibly take everything else with him. He carefully picked up the pure golden dagger, marvelled in the dim light at the precious diamond that artfully decorated it, and then stuck the treasure in the wide belt around his waist. Despite the limited time, he retrieved the golden dagger from his belt and looked at it again, wondering if it really had once belonged to Louis IX King of France.

With the golden dagger safely tucked away, and the large pockets of his trousers completely filled with jewellery and gold coins, Awaad found it difficult to move. Hesitant and undecided to depart, he closed the treasure and patiently waited in the room until he heard loud cheers that signified the conclusion of the circumcision ceremony. He walked slowly and melted into the happy crowd. At a considerable distance from the palace, Awaad hired the first donkey boy he encountered. He spotted Shookry and his son collecting money from family and guests as rewards for their successful performance.

The poor donkey moved much slower than usual as Awaad carried almost double his own weight in gold. The donkey boy could not understand it and whacked the beast a couple of times to no avail.

"It's all right. I'm not in any hurry anyway!" Awaad told the boy.

While riding slowly and at ease to his home, Awaad thought of himself as the new Ali Baba in town and wondered how he could return to his recently discovered treasure trove to empty it completely. Undoubtedly help is definitely needed, he thought, and whom can he trust. He certainly knew hundreds of people, yet only a handful whom he might consider qualified for the job. A few minutes before he reached his home, he thought of the one and only person that he would consider as courageous and trustworthy. He smiled as he very quietly uttered his old friend's name, "Mahroos!"

5

Populated mostly by farmers and a few artisans, El-Symbellawein is a small town located centrally in the delta. Known for its blossoming and lush fertile land, El-Symbellawein attracted many dedicated hard working farmers. Though they frequently suffered to a great extent from harsh and unregulated tax burdens, they were content and happy. They were also well known for their exceptional sense of humour and generosity. While food was plentiful, other necessary items had to be brought from nearby cities and particularly from Cairo. At least once a month, a group of merchants and travellers would arrange for a guarded caravan to Cairo. The caravan guards were usually Bedouin whose leader guaranteed a safe return for a fee or for a few commercial items. Sometimes to justify their high fees, the caravan leader pre-arranged a deal with charade highway robbers, mainly Bedouin from other tribes. Also at times, the guards would entice a few fake skirmishes with those robbers either on the way to or returning from Cairo. During these altercations, one or more guards would often pretend to have been badly injured to increase the pre-arranged protection fee. Surprisingly though, the travellers were no fools. They were quite aware of the deliberate clever game of deception. They pretended to take it all at face value and pay the required increased fees. In the end, everyone was happy!

Mahroos clearly heard the first call to prayers echoing from a nearby mosque and gleefully jumped out of bed. His excitement was not because he intended to perform the first of the five prayers a Muslim should do every day, but because he would be joining a caravan on its way to Cairo. Although he had not been to Cairo for almost ten years, had it not been an urgent request from his good old friend, Awaad, he would have never considered the trip. Knowing very well that his belongings were ready and perfectly packed, he stood in the middle of the room wondering what his next move should be. He turned and admired the uncovered delightful body of his stunning wife, Saneyya. While he stared at her amazing figure, many contradictory thoughts raced through his mind. Indeed, they had made love passionately the night before. Now, he was about to leave this beauty for a couple of weeks. He realized, with an ache in his heart, that he had never left her alone for such long periods of time since they had moved to El-Symbellawein. But then again, she was not alone with the children and three housekeepers for company. Well, in fact, she should be appreciative and grateful to him for making her a true lady of a large house on a farm with housekeepers and servants. He also thought that she should also be appreciative that he had never married a second, a third or, not to mention, a fourth wife. Saneyya was his one and only wife. Another idea hit him again as he considered that she should also be appreciative because he had never acquired concubines as many other rich men did. And so, he mumbled aloud to himself, "What are a couple of weeks away from her anyway, only a few weeks? Certainly she should understand and be thankful that I'll go through enough trouble just to find all the things she has asked me to bring her from Cairo." He then turned and looked at their two young daughters who were sleeping in an adjoining room and he smiled. As he was about to leave, he looked again at

Saneyya and could not simply resist the desire to hug and kiss her. Without any hesitation, he swiftly threw himself over her soft and delicate body and hailed her with kisses. Before she could realize what was happening, he was already inside her. As she began firing kisses at him, her arms held his lower waist as tightly as she could against her own.

Seemingly swimming in turbulent waters, they moved together fervently. As Saneyya was filled with joy and gasping for air, she managed to ask Mahroos, "What? Again!"

"I'm just making sure that you're still in love with me," he whispered in a lustful and husky voice.

The morning sun was about to rise when Mahroos at last left the house and hurriedly hired a donkey boy to bring him to the caravan. Once out of town, they arrived at a vast area where many caravans were separated by considerable distances from one another. A couple of boys stood in front of each caravan publicizing its destination. The donkey boy pointed at the caravan heading to Cairo. It was almost the largest one in the area. From afar, Mahroos could observe that the convoy organizers and their leader were engaged in a hot dispute with the chieftain of the Bedouin guards. Most travellers seemed weary and confused, especially the ones with women and children. When Mahroos drew closer and indicated his intention to join, one of the organizers approached him demanding the required departure fee that allowed him one saddle mount on a camel. Mahroos thought of his wife and children as he noticed that there were also a few other camels carrying what is known as *hawdag*, a saddle with a boxy tent secured at a camel's hump, and specially made to accommodate women and children.

From the top of the camel's hump, Mahroos noticed that an agreement had finally been reached. The Bedouin were divided into two groups, one at the head of the caravan while the other guarded the rear end. Meanwhile, the caravan leader arrogantly inspected his convoy from one end to the other then gave the signal to go. Following their leader, the caravan moved southward as a unit towards the eternal city of Cairo.

At the start of the procession, many travellers along the route silently recited verses from the Holy Koran and also uttered entreaties for their protection and safe return. On their way, whenever they approached a small village, dogs barked at them, little children asked for sweets, and elders offered them fresh water, smokes, coffee, and food in exchange for some coins. At prayer time, they stopped to unroll their special carpets to pray. At night, they erected their tents near a field hoping that the Bedouin would protect them from harm. Before they went to sleep, many travellers enjoyed smoking tobacco around a bonfire.

One night Mahroos joined a group of smokers who conversed generally about the trip and their lives. He did not say much but rather, he listened attentively to their conversation. Suddenly, the man next to him pointed at a Bedouin who was smoking near his camel.

"Look at that crazy Bedouin. He's sharing his smoke with his camel."

Mahroos asked in surprise, "How is that?"

"Look at what I mean. Look now!"

Mahroos noticed that the Bedouin filled his own lungs with tobacco smoke and then blew the smoke into the camel's nostrils.

"The camel seems to enjoy it," Mahroos said in surprise.

"Of course, the camel is enjoying it, which also means that the beast is just as addicted to tobacco as his Bedouin owner."

Mahroos took a long drag of the fine smoke and then blew it towards the starry sky.

"And what's wrong with that, anyway?" Mahroos asked in surprise.

"Haven't you heard the story of the Bedouin who was killed by his addicted camel? The camel craved tobacco at a time his owner could not provide. As a result, the camel crushed him dead to the ground."

"I hope that we all arrive safely before all the Bedouin are severely crushed by their own addicted camels."

A man who was listening to the conversation laughed as well, turned to Mahroos with an inquisitive look and said, "Do I know you from somewhere? I'm sure I remember meeting you."

"Yes, you're Ahmed Abboud the brother of Kamel Abboud from whom I bought my house and farm about ten years ago."

"Oh, yes! Your memory is better than mine. Are you headed for Cairo?"

Reluctantly, Mahroos continued the conversation as he remembered that he had paid more than he should have for the property.

"Yes, I have some friends to visit there. It should only be for a couple of weeks at the most."

"I'm only going there for business dealings. You see, I usually buy large quantities of clay pots of all sizes arriving on boats from producers in Upper Egypt, particularly from the town of Kena, where they have the best potters and clay in the country. Then I sell them to merchants of smaller establishments. Would you like to invest with me? It's a sure thing."

Mahroos replied, "My time is very limited and I've really never considered investing. If we meet again, I'll invite you for a coffee."

The man ended an uncomfortable conversation and then walked away.

After a few rough days, the impressive skyline of Cairo, with its tall minarets, appeared in the distance on the horizon. Happiness and jubilation filled the hearts of all travellers who unanimously thanked God fervently for their safe arrival without any harmful incidents. The caravan leader promptly announced that they would arrive at their destination near the grand market of Cairo for noon prayers. Cheers followed the announcement and praise for the courageous leader and his trusted team of good and loyal men. He appeared to be pleased and content with his success. He then concluded his announcement with warnings.

"Good people of El-Symbellawein, listen! The grand market of Cairo is a great place, but it's also full of clever thieves who can lift just about anything. Also, you'll encounter many clown beggars who are probably richer than some of you. God be with you all! For those who desire to return with us, we're leaving in two weeks at sunrise," the caravan leader announced.

Sighting Cairo again dazzled and excited Mahroos like a vulnerable adolescent. Certainly, it triggered many memories and experiences that he had had in that beloved City. Though he spent most if not all his life there and knew each and every corner of it, he felt like a complete stranger. He realized that all his French contacts were gone and that only a very few trustworthy friends remained. Had his dear friend, Awaad, not requested to see him, he would have never considered returning to Cairo. Suddenly, his mind went blank. All his dreams and plans about what to do and where to go had simply vanished. He felt helpless, insecure, and was abruptly possessed by an urge to return to his wife, Saneyya, and hold her in his arms.

6

After paying the caravan leader the balance of his travel fee, Mahroos felt totally exhausted. He realized that he needed at least one donkey boy to carry his belongings. Before he even attempted to look, five boys with their donkeys appeared in front of him from nowhere. Annoyed, Mahroos shook his head and in a commanding tone said, "I only need two of you!"

Two of the three boys stood their ground and persisted while the other three dragged their donkeys in defeat and left the scene. Mahroos rode one of the donkeys and the other beast carried his belongings. One of the boys asked for directions and Mahroos mentioned El Hussenia district. It was nearing late afternoon prayer time, the third prayer of the day in the Muslim world. *Muazzins*, those who call the faithful to prayers, were on top of minarets chanting their usual melodious calls reminding worshippers of their religious duties. Many people were heading for mosques while others, especially merchants, spread their prayer carpets beside or in front of their establishments to pray.

Mahroos had not been in Cairo for a few years yet he realized that much had not changed except that French soldiers were no longer roaming the streets. He wondered where they all were now, in France or in some other country, fighting again to control innocent people's lives. Many questions still occurred to him: *Why had they come to Egypt? Why had General Napoleon left them here only a year after their arrival?* Sure, he admired their women, made friends with many French soldiers, even with some high ranking officers, yet the puzzle still remained. *Why had they come here in the first place and remained for nearly three years?* What struck Mahroos most was the presence of Ottoman soldiers almost everywhere and that he could also see from their behaviour and facial expressions that they were up to no good wherever they went. While moving through the crowded lanes, he curiously asked one of the boys, "How're the Turks doing?"

"I wish that they would all go to hell and remain there. They're the worst crooks and sons of bitches you can imagine. They don't pay their fair share and recently we found one of us slaughtered and his donkey stolen."

"What makes you think that an Ottoman Turk had done it?" inquired Mahroos, pretending to be surprised.

"Only Ottoman Turks can get away with such a thing. The French, whom we used to call infidels, were kind and generous. Sometimes they even gave us more than we asked for. In fact, we try our best to avoid serving the Ottomans."

"God be with you fellows! We'll turn right here into the next lane."

"You're staying at Zeyad Abu Ali. His *kahn* (guesthouse) is well known and he is a great host. I must warn you though, he is expensive," said the other boy.

"Don't worry. He's an old friend and most likely he won't charge me a thing even if I stay forever."

The district they entered seemed more populated than any other they had been through before. For no apparent reason, people were somewhat anxious and in a hurry. Some merchants were in the process of closing their establishments. Before Mahroos could inquire about what was happening, the boys voluntarily told him that most likely the Ottoman soldiers were on their way to collect their protection dues from the merchants. As Mahroos and the boys were approaching the *kahn* of Zeyad Abu Ali, the two donkey boys exchanged secret signals to figure out Mahroos' ability to pay and how much they would charge him.

"Thanks, boys, for the good work. Just wait for a moment to see whether my host is present," Mahroos said.

One of the boys knocked at the door. A soft female voice answered, "Who is it?"

As the door opened slowly, they saw a stunningly beautiful woman who was partly visible from behind the huge wooden door. She wore a dark head scarf covering most of her black hair leaving in view just a little lock over her forehead. Her dazzling beautiful eyes gazed over the three in front of her and suddenly were focused only on Mahroos. Then, with a happy grin and a soft faraway tone she exclaimed, "Welcome, welcome, master Mahroos! We have been awaiting you all day. Come in, please."

Mahroos motioned the totally perplexed boys to bring his belongings past the door. The young boys were so taken and fascinated by the woman's beauty that they immediately moved his belongings inside and were about to leave in hasty excitement. "Aren't you boys forgetting something?" Mahroos asked.

They stopped, looked at each other, thanking God that they could turn and have a second glance at the beautiful woman. In the meantime and to their surprise, Mahroos stuck a silver coin with a value of a week's work in each of their hands. They gratefully thanked Mahroos, patted each other's shoulders, and quickly left.

The dazzling lady led Mahroos to a large sitting room. Countless pillows of different sizes were scattered on a marvellous Persian carpet. Female servants took his belongings to a room on the upper floor.

"Make yourself at home, master Mahroos. Master Zeyad Abu Ali is out and will be back shortly. Presently, we don't have many overnight guests and so if you need anything, please let me know," she whispered.

In the middle of the large room, Mahroos remained standing and mystified by the beauty and charm of his hostess.

"Would a cup of coffee and your pleasant company be too much to ask for?"

Her deep black eyes met his and a smile began to emerge on her face. She observed the servants as they walked briskly to a backroom at the end of a corridor and waited until the door was shut behind them. She then made one step towards Mahroos.

Mahroos asked, "What is your name besides the bright moon, healer of hearts, and most certainly, the one true beauty?"

Her eyes quickly moved away from his. Mahroos noticed her confusion. After a short pause, she glanced back at him and whispered, "Seaham is my name, but please don't tell anybody."

Mahroos took two steps backwards, while admiring her again.

"Seaham, after years of searching, I've finally found the most beautiful treasure on earth right before my eyes."

At this moment, the heavy front door opened with a creaking sound and they both realized that Zeyad Abu Ali was about to enter the house. Seaham rushed towards Mahroos gently touching his rigid body and kissing his cheek.

"At midnight I'll knock on your door three times," she whispered in his ear.

By the time Zeyad Abu Ali had reached the reception room, Seaham had vanished into a nearby hall while Mahroos sat comfortably on one of the large pillows.

"Welcome my friend! When did you arrive?" said Zeyad Abu Ali opening his arms to embrace Mahroos who got up to greet his friend.

"I'm sorry for not being able to receive you here, but the fact is that my wife is about to deliver a baby. I waited to know whether it were a boy or a girl. Then, the stupid midwife told me again for the fifth time that it's going to be tomorrow. For over a week she's been living in our house along with two of her helpers and every night she says, 'It is tomorrow.' What a real bitch! How's your family?"

Two female servants appeared with coffee and water-pipes. They served the two men politely and left.

"They're fine. Thank God, and, by the way, we're also expecting a new baby in a few months. Anyway, how's the great guesthouse doing? I don't see many patrons around."

"Well, after the French left, things weren't the way they used to be. Taxes were higher, Turks wanted everything for nothing, and the average clients went for the cheap." He paused a little, dragged ample smoke into his lungs from the water-pipe, and continued, "Yet I'm happy with my five servants, two cooks, and three exquisite hostesses. By the way, which one of them let you in?"

At this moment the three exquisite hostesses walked through the hallway leading to the reception room charmingly clothed in long semi-transparent outfits. Their uncovered hair descended below their shoulders and their dreamy eyes focused on Mahroos, the only guest in the room.

"Welcome, welcome, *ahlan, ahlan!*. It's my pleasure tonight to introduce you to our guest and my dear friend, master Mahroos. He has come all the way from El-Symbellawein to witness and enjoy your dazzling beauty and talents," Zeyad Abu Ali announced with a wide smile and a sense of happiness and pride.

Not used to such formalities, Mahroos felt a little uncomfortable and shifted his position on the pillow where he sat. Strangely enough, he felt a little embarrassed and shy, but as soon as his eyes met Seaham's, he was immediately himself again. After supper and a few delightful performances of singing and belly dancing, the three wonderful ladies retired to their quarters. Zeyad Abu Ali and Mahroos chatted a little more about their past adventures.

"Honestly, my dear friend, as you know, Awaad wants to see you urgently tomorrow afternoon at his old establishment. I'm sure you still remember where it is. He has been nagging me to send for you," Zeyad Abu Ali said.

"I knew it. Old Awaad again! I wonder what he wants this time. Anyway, I hope it's something worth the long trip I've made. How is he doing?"

"Well, same old Awaad. As far as I know, he owns eight establishments yet, as always, he still wants to get richer and wealthier all the time."

"Whatever the reason may be, I'll see him tomorrow," Mahroos replied.

"It's really great to see you. Frankly, the city is truly dull now and your presence here with us makes it a little more bearable. Also, don't forget that a week Thursday night, we're invited to a great celebration at Nassar Kamel *Bey*'s palace."

"Really! What's the occasion, if I may ask?" Mahroos inquired.

"Well, he and other Mamelukes will meet Mohammed Ali Pasha at the Citadel. That's the occasion. I'll let you know more tomorrow. Have a good night, my friend."

After Zeyad Abu Ali left and the last few candles were extinguished, a small dimly lit oil lamp was left in the reception hall. Tired, Mahroos went to his room, unpacked some of his belongings, and was about to go to bed when he heard three knocks at his door.

Before dawn, while all were floating in a world of dreams, Seaham quietly left Mahroos for her bedroom. Her body seemed to glow through her transparent silky gown against the dim light of the oil lamp that lit part of the room. Though the night was cool, she felt warm and wished for a swim in the Nile with Mahroos.

7

The following morning, Mahroos awoke fully rested. His exhausting trip of the last couple of days was now a thing of the past. He turned over and noticed that Seaham had left. He tried to collect his thoughts and realized that he should soon be on his way to meet his old friend, Awaad, whom he had actually come to Cairo to see. He wondered again why Awaad would want to meet with him after all these years. A few minutes before leaving his room, Mahroos heard knocks on his door and a female voice announced that breakfast was ready.

On his way to Awaad's operation, Mahroos noticed how the face of the city had changed. The kind of order the city somehow exhibited while the French were present had vanished. A ruthless grip by Ottoman soldiers seemed to affect the mood of the populace everywhere. He observed that people's behaviour and interactions reflected fear and distrust. Mahroos concluded that some evil was in the making and wished he could figure out what form it would take.

The two old friends met at the same place as they always had many times before. Though it had been almost ten years, Mahroos felt that it was just yesterday when he had been there. He looked with curious, examining eyes at his friend, Awaad, trying to discern any apparent changes in his features, but he could not find any. All he noticed was that his friend, despite his common attire and the dilapidated establishment he owned, was better off than he had imagined. Smiling to himself, he thought that the shabby establishment might be a cover up for wealth. Mahroos' mind recalled how he had actually made his fortune collecting gold and loot from Mameluke corpses on the night the French invaded and occupied Cairo. He could clearly visualize how the Mamelukes fell off their horses like flies while trying to defend the city against a modern well-trained French army. That battle became known by Napoleon's army as the Battle of the Pyramids. Though, at the time, it was the Ottomans' duty to defend the country they occupied, they cowardly had not. Instead, the Mamelukes, who were not in charge, fought valiantly and lost. His thoughts were suddenly interrupted by Awaad's rough voice.

"The new Pasha seems at ease with the Mamelukes. He has allowed many to remain and live in Cairo despite the tension between them and his Ottoman soldiers. I find that odd, don't you?"

"What have we got to do with that? They may all burn in hell forever. Do you think I care?" exclaimed Mahroos.

"He even invited them to the Citadel to celebrate his son's departure to fight in Arabia."

"I couldn't care less anyway about all their invitations or celebrations. Zeyad Abu Ali has been invited to a celebration and he asked me to join him. What has that to do with me or with us anyway?"

"Well, it has a lot to do with us and I'll explain. But first of all, my dear friend, have a good long drag of smoke from this unique *goza* which I have prepared especially for this occasion."

Mahroos wondered a little, and then realized that a little hashish with an old friend would be all right and, in fact, he could actually take more than one long drag from it. He inhaled into his lungs a considerable amount of smoke, held it for a short while, and then slowly exhaled. He then gazed at Awaad and smiled, expecting one of his old jokes.

"Lately, I have acquired a magnificently studded golden dagger. I mean a truly pure gold dagger which, I believe, belonged to Louis the Ninth, the old King of France, who was captured and imprisoned in Mansoura. That's not all, my friend. I've also got many other valuable items including countless gold coins."

Awaad stopped for a moment to see Mahroos' reaction to all that. While waiting, he noticed a new inquisitive seriousness showing on his friend's face.

"In fact," he continued, "there's a lot of stuff still waiting where that dagger came from, more booty than you can ever imagine. Frankly, there is enough gold there to sink several boats deep down into the Nile."

Mahroos asked eagerly, "And where's all that supposed to be? Buried in a cave somewhere in the desert? And how many others have you already told about that mysterious treasure of yours?"

"I've told no one since I trust no one. Surely, I could do it alone again a second time. But I'm convinced that a third time would never cross my mind."

A moment of silence passed. The only sound was bubbling water from both coconut shells of their *gozas* and those of other patrons.

Mahroos questioned in surprise, "Well, if you say that you can do it alone again, then why are you telling me?"

"The reason I'm telling you all this is simply because you're the one and only person I can trust." He blew a giant cloud of smoke in the air, then continued, "The idea of doing it with you and not alone is simply because, undoubtedly, two can carry a lot more than one."

Awaad looked around at his nearly empty establishment to make sure no one was listening.

"Now, and before I go any further and give you more specifics about why, where, how, and when, I first need a definite and binding commitment from you. What do you say?"

Mahroos asked, "If I take what I can carry and you take whatever you're able to handle then what're you gaining from taking me along?"

"I've never said that you'll take all what you can carry. What I may tell you now is that you'll get a fair share of the big loot. Trust me. You'll never regret it unless we both die in the process. Now, are you in or would you rather go back home?"

"Die in the process? I didn't come all the way here to die in any process."

"No, you won't die. Don't be afraid, my friend. You won't die. I promise."

Mahroos asked suspiciously, "Then what exactly would my share be?"

"You'll get one half of what you can carry. Now, no more questions unless you tell me that you're in," Awaad replied.

Mahroos was about to ask why only one half when he realized that Awaad was already annoyed. He looked Awaad in the eyes.

"I'm in! You can count on me, old friend."

"Somehow I knew you wouldn't disappoint me. Welcome to our last adventure! And now, here are answers to some of your questions. The other half of what you're able to carry will go to an old man who informed me about that treasure. He's from Baghdad and he told me that many generations ago, his grandfather built the storage room with a magic handle."

Mahroos interrupted with a weary smile, "I thought we'd talk about gold not an old guy from Baghdad with a magic handle! How in the world will you bring his share to Baghdad? How do you know that he's still alive?"

"Now, you don't want to listen to any detail. The treasure, as you call it, is in a palace that belongs to an *Emir*. Come to meet me here on Friday with a long strong rope wrapped and hidden around you waist."

"Is it Nassar Kamel *Bey*'s palace? That's where I'm going for the celebration with Zeyad Abu Ali."

"No, it isn't. You just be vigilant and well-rested before coming here a week Friday. As you know, we have a lot in common. I really wish that one day I could settle down and lead a quiet life like you," Awaad stated in a sincere tone.

"You can always do that, my friend,"

Awaad suddenly looked even more serious and as if he had another important issue to bring up. "Now, my friend, there is a favour that I would like to ask you and hope that you're able to achieve it."

"For a reasonable price, I'll achieve anything," Mahroos said jokingly.

Awaad continued with earnestness, "Earlier I made reference to a pure golden dagger, magnificently studded which may have once belonged to Louis the Ninth, King of France."

"Yes, I remember. If you think that I would be interested in buying, forget it right now."

"When will you ever learn to be patient? I haven't even finished my sentence and you've already reached a conclusion."

"All right! Let's hope it's a short sentence then." Mahroos finally noticed the seriousness on his friend's face and regretted his silly remarks, then in complete sincerity added, "Well, forgive me, I'm listening."

Awaad stopped speaking while a waiter refreshed their *gozas.*

"Do you remember a civilian French man who became a Muslim, married a widower, and worked at Al-Azhar? He also spoke fluent Arabic and memorized the Holy Koran."

"Well, if you're referring to Monsieur Dumont, or who is now known as Al Sayed Abd Elkareem, of course I know him. Even though I haven't seen him for some years, I'm sure he's still my friend. What has he got to do with all that?"

"Obviously, the golden dagger is a ceremonial object and not meant to be used in combat. It has some strange inscription on it. I copied it on paper as accurately as I possibly could, yet no one was able to decipher any of it except the name of Louis the Ninth, King of France."

"Why worry about the inscription when you've got the gold? Whatever the meaning may be, it won't bring you more money, believe me."

"It isn't about the gold or the money. It's about the significance and implication of it."

"You've gone crazy, my friend. I don't even know what you're talking about. I, myself, need someone to explain to me what you mean by the significance and implication of it."

"Look here! Just to give you an idea. When the French found a Pharaoh's stone in Rosetta with three ancient inscriptions on it, they treated it like a gold mine. When the French capitulated, the English insisted on having the stone for themselves and allowed the French to have only a replica of it. Believe me, they would have gone to war over it." Awaad could see the puzzlement on Mahroos' face and yet he continued, "There are so many things around us of greater value than gold, my dear friend."

Mahroos said mockingly, "Sure! Sure! Inscriptions! Oh yeah! What do you want me to do, go to Rosetta and bring you a stone?"

"No, just take this paper to your old friend, Monsieur Dumont, and see if he can make some sense out of it."

On the way back to the *kahn* or guesthouse and despite his wealth, Mahroos actually felt excited about the prospect of being involved again in an adventure with Awaad. Yet, deep in his soul, he felt cheerless because even with all the wealth he might be able to accumulate, unlike the Mamelukes or the Ottoman Turks, he must continue to lead a discreet and dull life. Sadly, he couldn't even ride a magnificent horse or wear extravagant clothes. He must be content with a tiny piece of land

and a modest house. Otherwise, tax collectors, Turks, or Mamelukes would be after him to collect or even take it all away.

Back at the *kahn* he asked the servants to fill the tub in his room with hot water. Once the last servant had left the room and he was about to undress, he heard the three distinct knocks at his door.

8

Napoleon's invasion of Egypt was only a part of an irresistible dream to build an empire beyond India. To make Egypt a favourable and constructive colony for France, a scientific team with a wide range of specialists in almost every field accompanied his army to analyze and study the country. Alas, dreams do not always come true; however, the scientific team of nearly a hundred men emerged with much more success which had a lasting effect on Egypt than that of the entire army.

Monsieur Dumont, or Al Sayed Abd Elkareem, as he was commonly known in Cairo after embracing Islam, had been married to Hameeda for over ten years. Their marriage ceremony was conducted by one of Al-Azhar's highly-regarded Sheiks and attended by a few relatives and friends. Naturally, the Islamic law was fully observed in all aspects of the wedding and, of course, a lavish feast highlighted the celebration.

Together with his wife Hameeda, they lived happily in her house. His fluency in Arabic and his understanding of the Islamic religion and culture were all now put into practice. After quitting his savant position with Napoleon's army, he secured a researcher post at the virtuous Al-Azhar Mosque, the center of Islamic studies. He wore Turkish attire, prayed five times a day, and joined each Friday prayer at a mosque. Despite his French origin, he soon became well-respected and appreciated by many of his Egyptian neighbours, who began to treat him as a true brother in Islam.

His love and appreciation for Hameeda was increasing every day and sometimes he wondered how he had ever managed to live without her. At night, she was the sensual woman he had always wished and longed for. During the day, she was the companion, the friend, and the intellectual in whose company he took enormous pleasure. He always thought that Egypt was where he really belonged. He also believed that, in Cairo, possibilities for an educated civilian were quite endless. Almost each year, he and his wife Hameeda would spend their summer vacation in France and his sister, Carole, would occasionally come from Paris and visit them in Cairo.

Before Hameeda fell in love and married Monsieur Dumont, she comfortably lived alone in her two-floor home near Al Ezbakeya Square. Though she was originally raised in a small village, her broad-minded father insisted on her private education at home. She, therefore, was one of a few women in Cairo who could read, write, and recite the Koran. For a variety of reasons, at first she had refused several proposals to remarry after her first husband had died years earlier. At forty, her body was still slender and she had always had a youthful and attractive appearance. Her lively disposition radiated confidence and reassurance and made those she met accept and trust her. Hameeda enjoyed a regular and splendid income as she had inherited several agricultural farms from both her husband and her father. The farms were administered by one of her brothers who, on occasion, came to visit and deliver the proceeds. Although she had four female servants and an elderly doorman to perform all the chores of her large home, she occasionally enjoyed cooking.

Naturally-gifted as an entrepreneur, she managed a number of businesses that yielded her considerable additional earnings. Though a lot of money was made from such activities, she regarded her dealings as an amusing and exciting pastime. Blessed with a healthy body and boundless energy, she spent her days relishing what she enjoyed doing. One of her favorite activities was buying and selling women's jewellery among her ever-growing circle of friends and acquaintances. Applying the very basic principles of economics, jewellery was bought at a low price from those who needed cash and sold at a higher value to those who wanted it. Sellers as well as buyers respected her and tremendously appreciated her services.

To Hameeda, however, her delight was centered on endless friendly discussions with others and in applying her clever haggling and bargaining skills. She adored entertaining and being entertained by harmless chitchats and chatters. Regardless of the purpose of her visits, she entered assuredly many homes and was accepted by all as a trusted member of the family. Highly esteemed and respected by many Cairene families, Hameeda's list of qualifications included the title of matchmaker. Out of passion and good will, she helped connect many families through the marriage of their sons or daughters. Although she was rewarded handsomely each time, her true intentions were simply to facilitate contacts. When sometimes questions emanated regarding a dowry or certain procedures, her opinions were certainly welcomed. When she matched the son of a well-known merchant with the daughter of a wealthy landowner, her fame as a matchmaker reached its peak. Due to her knowledge of *sharia* or Islamic law, she assisted many families in drafting and writing marriage contracts, wills, and clarified the complex laws of inheritance.

With fewer social activities and business undertakings, Hameeda devoted her life to her husband, Monsieur Dumont. She enjoyed tremendously travelling with him to France and other

European countries. She always welcomed her sister-in-law's visits. She also appreciated Carole's respect for local customs and adherence to the conservative dress code.

*****

When Monsieur Dumont entered the reception hall, he enthusiastically received his old friend, Mahroos. It had been almost ten years ago when they had last seen each other.

"Welcome to Cairo, my dear friend. When did you arrive? Of course, you'll have supper with us. The servants are preparing a room for you and your wife. Where is she?"

"Well, I'm very happy to see you, Al Sayed Abd Elkareem," said Mahroos.

Suddenly, Monsieur Dumont's wife, Hameeda, entered the room, greeted Mahroos then asked, "Where is Saneyya and the children. Haven't they come?"

"No. They're not with me. I'm sorry. Next time I'll bring them. I have only one question for Al Sayed Abd Elkareem and then I really should go," Mahroos replied shyly and in a hesitant manner.

"Give my love to Saneyya and the children for me," answered Hameeda as she left the room.

"Yes I will." Mahroos then turned to Al Sayed Abd Elkareem and said, "A friend of mine would like to know the meaning of this writing, if possible. It is very important for him to know the meaning of what the inscription says."

With shaky hands, Mahroos took a paper out of his pocket and handed it to Monsieur Dumont.

"Oh, Coptic script? And what has Louis the Ninth, King of France to do with Coptic script?"

Mahroos asked in confusion, "With what, Al Sayed Abd Elkareem?"

"What I mean, Mahroos, is that Louis the Ninth, King of France is the name written here yet he was not a Copt. He was certainly a Christian but most certainly never belonged to the Coptic church of Egypt. You see, the Coptic Church was founded in Egypt and not in France. Therefore, I believe that Louis the Ninth had nothing to do with this Coptic inscription. If it were in Latin or French, I would certainly say that there was some connection."

Perplexed, Mahroos asked, "What does the writing really say?"

"Well, it simply says, 'The Father, the Son, and the Holy Spirit' in Coptic characters."

"And so, what do I tell my friend?"

"Tell him what I just said!"

"Yes, Coptic characters, 'The Father, the Son, and the Holy Spirit.'"

"Perfect! And when are you going back to your family, Mahroos?"

"I believe in a week or so."

After an uneasy conversation with Monsieur Dumont, Mahroos was about to excuse himself to report the findings to Awaad when Hameeda re-entered the reception with another extraordinarily beautiful woman next to her. The woman seemed European but garbed in local, conservative clothes. Mahroos was puzzled and regretted having refused to stay for supper. He began to wonder who this woman was and what she was doing at Monsieur Dumont's home.

"Mahroos, I would like you to meet Carole, my husband's sister," Hameeda said in a quiet manner while smiling at the baffled Mahroos.

"I'm really happy to be here, really happy to meet your sister. She's not Egyptian but she looks like an Egyptian," Mahroos commented while looking at the attractive woman. He thought that he must find a way to stay a little longer at least to get to know more about her.

Monsieur Dumont added, "Carole loves Egypt and this is her fourth visit with us from France. Are you sure, Mahroos, that you won't reconsider joining us for supper?"

"Yes, yes, I'll reconsider. I'm hungry. I think I'll stay for supper. Thank you. Thank you. I'm truly hungry now."

While they were having coffee after supper, Carole casually said to Mahroos in Arabic yet with a distinct French accent, "I heard a lot about you from my brother and my sister-in-law."

"Yes, they know me very well. I've been their friend for many years. Carole, you like Egypt?"

"Of course! I adore Egypt."

"Mahroos, we have a favour to ask you and I hope it won't interfere in any way with your plans while in Cairo," Monsieur Dumont added expectantly.

"Just ask me anything. It is always a delight to do it," Mahroos smiled and looked at the three of them excitedly.

"As I mentioned earlier, this is Carole's fourth visit and, for some reason or other, we postponed her visit each time to the Step Pyramid at Saqqara. Unfortunately, this time my wife and I are very busy and I thought ...."

Mahroos interrupted with excitement and said, "Of course, I could take her there right now. I'm quite sure. No problem!"

Carole replied softly, "Not right now, Monsieur Mahroos, perhaps tomorrow morning."

9

When Lazoughly and Saleh Koosh were finally alone in a guestroom at Lazoughly's palace, they were troubled and irritated. Extremely loyal and close confidants of Mohammed Ali Pasha, they realized that only they and Taher Pasha, the commander of the Albanian unit of the Ottoman army, vaguely knew about some scheme devised by the Pasha to purge the Mamelukes. They were beset by terror and fear as serious trouble could erupt anytime and anywhere. Their burden seemed much larger than anticipated in the sense that they not only had to keep their knowledge highly secret but they also had to invite the Mamelukes to attend an exceedingly elaborate celebration. Through intricate backchannels, the two men were also expected to finance what had to appear as spontaneous festivities for the general population. All must be done with the most perfectly orchestrated craftiness.

For a good while, the two men sat facing one another in complete silence. Their thoughts were concise and clear yet expressing them certainly needed an exceptional choice of words and language. Both fully understood well the tasks ahead of them together with all the necessary procedures. Suddenly, Lazoughly stood up and made sure that the door was closed and then turned to his mate, "With all due respect, we should have inquired more about how the Pasha plans to eliminate them. We definitely know that something will take place but, my dear friend, we are completely baffled."

"Well, for once I agree with you; however, in a way, I'm quite satisfied with that. Remember, we're not involved in the actual elimination process. Don't you think? It isn't our job."

"I fully understand. All I'm saying is that, at the least, we should know when and how the deed will be done."

"You know that the Pasha is a very cautious man not only by nature but also because the Mamelukes plotted several times in the past to assassinate him. Even a few weeks ago, an attempt was made on his life while he was inspecting a newly-built fleet in Suez. I believe that this is obviously his response."

"This is not a simple matter. If we're to participate, we should know each and every detail all the way."

"Frankly, I don't want to know. If you're so eager, why didn't you ask him?"

"I thought he would voluntarily open up to us."

"Remember, each and everything, which he has ever planned, went exactly the way he had wanted it. He succeeded in every plot he formulated. That Pasha knows how and, as always, he gets it perfectly done. Believe me!"

"How can he eliminate the Mamelukes during a parade? I simply can't imagine that."

"Well, they attempted to assassinate him and they won't get away with it so easily."

"I'm certainly curious about how he'll do it. Now, let's plan our own part."

"Yes, of course. Well I believe that, depending on the power and prestige of each *Emir* or Mameluke *Bey,* either we personally invite him on behalf of the Pasha or we send an envoy with the invitation."

"All must be respectable and follow a friendly protocol and certainly we would beg them, if needed."

"Those envoys, sent to low-ranking Mamelukes, must be instructed on how to be very polite and considerate no matter what the responses or reactions might be."

"Indisputably, that's absolutely necessary. We don't want any apparent misgivings about our hospitality and decent intentions."

"Well then, I believe that street festivities would be a much simpler task."

"To me that's a non-issue. My men will have food stalls all over the city and will also engage dancers and musicians. The whole city will be living in a fantasy world."

"Tomorrow, my scribe will prepare a list of all the high ranking *Emirs,* Mameluke *Beys* and, of course, will send special messengers to announce our visits."

"Do you think they will all accept the invitation?"

"I don't see why they wouldn't. Most have been in Cairo for over a year and despite some skirmishes here or there, I would say they've done very well here. Why would any of them refuse to attend?"

"Excellent! I'll see you tomorrow in my best attire, even if I have to import a new set from Istanbul."

*****

A day later, proudly in their ceremonial dress along with an entourage of officials from the Pasha's court, Lazoughly and Saleh Koosh announced themselves at *Emir* Moustafa El-Gandour's palace. They were led respectfully and courteously into the magnificent reception hall and were politely informed that the *Emir* would join them shortly. Delighted by the splendid welcome, Lazoughly and Saleh Koosh smiled at each other reassuringly and, in their minds, began rehearsing the invitation protocol as planned. Mysteriously, they both felt that the Pasha's sharp and watchful eyes were focused on them and that only a positive outcome would be expected of them. Their distressful thoughts were interrupted when *Emir* Moustafa El-Gandour entered the hall and greeted them warmly. From both sides, streams of complimentary words flowed and kind expressions became the subject of dialogue. Despite the historical tension between the two sides, a sense of trust and ease began to prevail among them. Obviously, Lazoughly saw the opportunity to present his invitation to the Citadel while at the same time Saleh Koosh was preparing himself to intervene when or if necessary.

"Presently and, as you may imagine, Mohammed Ali Pasha has various challenges on his hands," Lazoughly began. "Otherwise, he would personally be here instead of us."

Emir Moustafa El-Gandour looked at both men in surprise and wondered what the Pasha would be doing here had he not been as occupied as they had claimed. It may be wise, he thought, to listen attentively in complete calmness to what the two envoys had to say.

"It is indeed an honour for us to speak on behalf of the Pasha," Lazoughly continued. "We are inviting you as well as all *Emirs* and Mamelukes to attend and participate in the celebration and the farewell procession of the Pasha's son, Touson, before leading his army to war in Arabia. The celebration and the procession throughout the city shall start from the Citadel where the Pasha personally will be expecting all of you. Your presence will irrefutably bequeath a great honour on Mohammed Ali Pasha and the entire Ottoman Empire, as well."

Though Moustafa El-Gandour remained silent with his eyes fixed on the two men, his thoughts began to question the sincerity and truthfulness of what he had heard. He then realized that he should give some kind of reply that would seem neither reassuringly positive nor completely negative.

"Thank you, gentlemen, with the utmost honour and delight, I have received the Pasha's message of invitation. As it appears, it is not only a personal invitation to me but also meant for many others, as well. Therefore, we shall give it our utmost priority and consideration. In due time, of course, our messenger shall convey our reply."

10

Early the following morning, a well-groomed Mahroos was on his way to Monsieur Dumont's house. Proud to be able to take Carole on a trip to the Step Pyramid of Saqqara, he walked swiftly towards a donkey stall. A few donkey boys ran to him but he only pointed at two boys whose donkeys had better saddles and roared, "Follow me!"

One of the boys asked, "Do you want to ride, master?"

"Not now! Just follow me as I said."

Mahroos stuck a jug of water into one saddle and a few sacks filled with sweetmeats into the other. He knew that it was not going to be easy yet he was thrilled by the idea of accompanying Carole.

They stopped at Monsieur Dumont's house, and as Mahroos was just about to knock, the doorkeeper opened the door, "Master Al Sayed Abd Elkareem is not available but Lady Carole is expecting you, master Mahroos. Come in please."

Mahroos' mind dazed with wild imagination at the thought of Carole being alone in the house waiting for him. He immediately thought of dismissing the donkey boys, but as he looked into the courtyard, he spotted Carole standing and ready to go. She was perfectly dressed like a well-to-do conservative Egyptian lady. Despite her local head cover, her beautiful face was amazingly bright under the morning sun. Her controlled yet welcoming smile and naturally relaxed attitude gave Mahroos a sense of comfort and ease.

"Good morning! You're perfectly on time, Monsieur Mahroos."

Mahroos was thrilled to hear Carole's greeting in Arabic with her delightful French accent. She walked briskly past him to the open gate and stood near one of the donkeys.

For a moment, Mahroos was amazed by her beauty and perfectly shaped body then suddenly said, "Believe me, I could have stayed all night by the door to be even more perfectly on time to see you."

"Monsieur Mahroos, wait all night by the door! Isn't that a bit much? Are these donkeys for us? Can I ride that one?"

"Of course you can."

A donkey boy attempted to assist Carole but Mahroos pushed him aside and gave him an angry look. He then held Carole's hand, touched her tiny waist, and lifted her up on the saddle. Blood rushed through his body as he remembered his old devilish days in Cairo. He realized that his good friend, Monsieur Dumont, had entrusted him with his sister and that he must not be tempted to take advantage of such trust. With her eyes focused on his, Carole thanked him with a smile that made his head spin. Again, he pushed the donkey boy aside and, for a good while, he walked while dragging the harness of her donkey. Once out of the city, he mounted his donkey and rode next to her. The two boys followed them at a distance. In a little over an hour, it became warmer as the sun filled the clear bright skies. They reached a small village and could see the Sphinx and the three Pyramids of Giza on the horizon. They decided to stop for refreshments and rest for a while near the tent of a coffee stand. While sipping their coffee and eating their sweets, their eyes met and they exchanged smiles.

Carole asked, "Where is Dar-Abu-Arab?"

"What? I've never heard that name before. Why do you ask?"

Looking at Mahroos, Carole answered in a stern and determined manner.

"Because that's where I really want to go."

"What? I thought that we were going to the Step Pyramid at Saqqara."

"That's what I said yesterday. Today, I want to go to Dar-Abu-Arab. It's a village not very far from here. Would you take me there, please?"

Bewildered and troubled Mahroos was surprised by her sudden request. He could not understand her abrupt shift of mood and her intention to go to a place he did not even know. He quickly tried to think of a reason for such a change but could not come up with an answer. He looked at her face and failed in trying to formulate some response. Suddenly it hit him. She must have a lover waiting for her there, he concluded. He got up and immediately said, "We're leaving now."

"Leaving, where to?"

"Back to your brother's house, that's where to," Mahroos answered firmly.

"What? To the house! I told you where I want to go."

"Where you want to go is one thing and my responsibility to your brother is another. If you think that I'll take you to go to bed with some son of a bitch while I wait for you like a pimp, you're absolutely mistaken. Get on your damn beast. We're all going back."

"Monsieur Mahroos, I thought that you were a gentleman. With those accusations and language, are you speaking to me? If you think that we must go back home, then so be it. But the least you could do, as a true gentleman, is to listen to me first before drawing conclusions."

"I came to my conclusions because I can read minds," Mahroos retorted.

"Well, Monsieur Mahroos, my mind is French and you can't even speak French, let alone read it. Would you be kind enough to just listen to me, please?"

Somehow, Mahroos felt a little awkward. He tossed a coin at one of the donkey boys and asked him to order a water-pipe. Then he turned to Carole pretending to be troubled and said, "Where is Dar-Abu-Arab anyway? And whom do you want to see there?"

"I don't know where Dar-Abu-Arab is. All I know is that it's near Saqqara. Secondly, I don't know anybody there. All I want is to buy something, which, to my knowledge, is only available there," Carole said almost in tears.

Regretting his harsh response and softening his tone, Mahroos responded, "Carole, I could buy you anything you want from Cairo. Why did we come all the way here to Saqqara when it's not even Saqqara you want but Dar-Abu-Arab? Cairo has everything, don't you think? What is it you really want to buy?"

"Mummies! Ancient Egyptians Mummies! That's exactly what I want and, if possible, in powder form."

"What? Mummies! What in hell do you need Mummies for? I can't believe what I'm hearing! Mummies, you say, possibly in powder form? Are you sure?"

"Yes, I'm sure. Chemists in France and all over Europe use the powder as a medicine for all kinds of ailments. Besides helping to alleviate human suffering, I can also make a lot of money selling it to chemists. Believe me! It's in great demand there. All I need are a few fragments of Mummies crushed into powder to take with me back to France."

The donkey boy returned with a fresh water-pipe. Mahroos took a few long drags of smoke into his lungs, then blew the smoke up into the air and started a long bellowing laugh. He realized that he could not stop laughing aloud and handed the water-pipe back to the boy. He held his stomach trying, somehow, to stifle his uncontrollable convulsive sounds. After a few minutes, he managed to sit a little more subdued on the sandy ground. He then looked at a puzzled Carole and exclaimed, "Which comes to you first: alleviate human suffering or a lot of money from Mummies?"

A period of complete silence ensued. Finally, the silence was interrupted by suppressed weeping and sobbing from Carole. Her enormous disappointment in Mahroos was quite visible. All hopes to accomplish what she had come to Egypt for were gone. Help on this matter could never be expected neither from her brother nor from his wife, Hameeda. Now her last hope in Mahroos had just ended. While a stream of tears trickled down her delicate face, she quietly mounted her donkey without any assistance and waited.

Mahroos inquired calmly, "Where are you going?"

"There's no longer anything I want. Would you be so kind as to accompany me home?"

"I'm so sorry for my stupid reaction. Please accept my regrets and sorrow. Allow me one minute to ask the owner about Dar-Abu-Arab."

A few minutes later, Mahroos reappeared and stated, "Dar-Abu-Arab is about an hour from here. I was also warned that the people there are strange and cruel. The good news for you, my dear Carole, is that I know how to deal with such folks."

"Do you really want to take me there?"

"Wherever you want to go! I'll even take you to the moon," Mahroos said with a gentle smile.

11

Unlike others in the city, *Emir* Moustafa El-Gandour's palace was regarded as the most luxurious. With a reception hall that defied all others, *Emir* Moustafa El-Gandour decided to invite all the leading *Emirs* and Mamelukes of Cairo to discuss and debate an invitation that they had received from Mohammed Ali Pasha, the Governor of Egypt. Coming from the official representative of the Ottoman Sultan, such an invitation could not simply be rejected or ignored by the Mamelukes. Despite their differences, it was important that a consensus be reached and abided by.

As anticipated, they all arrived in their most ostentatious style and traditional elegance. They were welcomed and served in the magnificent reception hall. After an elaborate exchange of compliments, they waited for their host, *Emir* Moustafa El-Gandour, to begin the debate. When he arrived, he greeted them all with a warm welcome. One *Emir* eagerly raised his hand, stood up, and began his argument: the debate had begun.

Emir Mohssen Elkarawany vigorously and convincingly told the nearly one hundred and fifty leading Mameluke *Emirs* who had gathered, "Think about it! Yes, dear brothers, think about it! You ought to understand and value each and every word I say! I wouldn't even consider this invitation for all the gold in this world. Listen to me, my friends. Personally, I don't trust being near that fox, Mohammed Ali, even after he's dead and gone. You, of all people, expect me to accept his invitation? Just ask yourselves where is he inviting us? Where, to the Citadel, in his own den? Wake up, brothers! Wake up, friends! I repeat. Mohammed Ali is evil, immoral, and a master of deception and I can list a lot more descriptive names for him. My final answer is an unconditional, absolute, no, no, no! There is one more important thing. Please don't think that someday you might be able to reassess or lament this unwise decision of yours because, regrettably, you won't have the luxury of being around to do so!"

Another *Emir* raised his hand, stood up, and placed his coffee cup on a silver tray next to him. He first gazed at his audience to make sure he had their undivided attention before his voice echoed loudly in the hall.

"Have you all forgotten that only a few months ago we were at war with him throughout Upper Egypt? Have you?" Again, he stared at the seated crowd and then continued, "Of course, he retreated but definitely not because we had won." He observed the crowd intensely and then proceeded, "He retreated because the English had sent a fleet to Alexandria to support us. He retreated in order to fight the English." His voice rose as he lamented, "It is painful to say that. Had he stayed, we would have been totally crushed and, of course, we wouldn't be here to discuss his irreverent invitation." He paused for a while, then offered, "Here's the point I want to make, my dear fellows. Certainly the English had no trouble capturing Alexandria. But when the English moved to Rosetta and thought that the town was unguarded, the Ottoman soldiers attacked and defeated them not face to face like fighting men, but rather by ambushing them from behind windows and rooftops of civilian homes. Mohammed Ali and his soldiers are not to be trusted. First, he will make you feel safe and then savagely stab you when you least expect it."

Exceptionally well-dressed Zafaran *Bey* stood up, thanked *Emir* Moustafa El-Gandour for his great hospitality, extended his gratitude to all the *Emirs* for their presence, and then began to address his fellow *Emirs* in a calm and steady tone.

"How many *Emirs* and Mamelukes were lately ambushed, robbed, and killed by Mohammed Ali's Ottoman soldiers? How many evil plots and deceptions were wickedly launched by his supporters? I'm sure that you're all aware of most, if not all, such depressing and gloomy events. Remember, we have been invited to celebrate his son's departure to fight a war in Arabia. That's the Sultan's war and the Ottomans' war but definitely not ours. Why should we celebrate? Let's all anticipate and pray for their destruction and defeat in Arabia. Then, and only then, may we truly rejoice and celebrate. "

Arguments and counter arguments regarding acceptance or rejection of Mohammed Ali's proposed invitation continued by other *Emirs*. Most were persuasively valid yet none brought about a consensus among those present. Disdainful heckling followed each speech and the odd occasional fistfight or name calling became common. A respectful calm overcame the assembly when *Emir* Moustafa El-Gandour, the host, at last stood up, raised his right hand, and quietly addressed the group, "Dear brothers!" He waited a little to make sure that all eyes and ears were directed at him. Then he began his well prepared speech.

"Please permit me to thank all of you for accepting my invitation without debating it first!" The *Emirs* started to laugh loudly and then returned to full attention. *Emir* Moustafa El-Gandour resumed his speech in an even tone, "The question we should be asking ourselves is not whether to accept or reject Mohammed Ali's invitation. The real question, my dear brothers, would perhaps be: What advantages and benefits await us as *Emirs* of this land? True, a few years ago Mohammed Ali was fiercely fighting us in Upper Egypt. Undoubtedly, his objectives were to parade all our heads mounted on spears and display them for public viewing at the Citadel square. Surprisingly and recently, we are now permitted to come and live in Cairo with our families and friends. Today, we can walk the streets of Cairo without animosity or serious clashes with his loyal Albanian soldiers. Well, dear friends, does that mean that I trust him? The answer is definitely and positively *No!* Mohammed Ali is a cunning and deceitful enemy. I can smell his hatred for all of us not only here but also everywhere I go."

At that moment, the hall fell into complete silence in anticipation of what the consensus might be. They regarded the speaker attentively as one of their great leaders whose views they valued and respected.

Emir Moustafa El-Gandour persisted, "What is beneficial to us? That is my question to you. I'm not here to tell you to accept or reject Mohammed Ali's invitation. I am here merely to clarify the situation. The final decision is unquestionably yours. Let's examine the situation now. Mohammed Ali's great army is out of Cairo and about to sail the Red Sea to Arabia. Only a symbolic unit remains here for his son's parade out of the city. In a few days, his entire army will be out of the country obviously leaving him defenseless and unprotected. That is why I suspect he invited us and that is why he wants our friendship and trust. He wants to appease us while his forces are fighting a war imposed upon him by the Sultan in Constantinople, to pacify us while his army is unavailable to protect him. If we don't accept his invitation, we may be regarded as either cowards or unappreciative. If we don't go, we may then be regarded as opponents and foes. If we play our role correctly, we may attain some trust for now, and then when the time is right, we may forcefully strike. Remember, the fact that Mohammed Ali has formally invited us and that reality alone makes us formally and officially his guests. According to all traditions, we should not only be respectfully treated and generously served but also our safety and protection must consequently be guaranteed." *Emir* Moustafa El-Gandour waited, had a sip from a glass of rosewater, and further offered, "I have a plan, my dear brothers. In a few weeks, I'll invite him to this grand hall. The rest of the plan, dear friends, I'll leave to your imagination."

Around low, elegantly decorated tables covered with a wide variety of food, the *Emirs* sat in small groups of eight or ten in the great reception hall. Numerous, colourful Persian rugs, and many decorative pillows were scattered everywhere for comfort and added to the richness of the decor. For a short while, after the host concluded his argument, a strange silence filled the hall. Then gradually the *Emirs* began to discuss and debate among themselves whether they should accept or reject Mohammed Ali's invitation. Their emotions were high and expressed by facial and hand gestures. At times, one *Emir* or another would become angry and move away from a table while gesturing discontent or revulsion. After an hour of debate and heated discussions, civility was restored with smiles and chuckles. Unexpectedly, a group of seven male and four female musicians quietly walked into the magnificent hall and sat in designated places. Their leader, an elder, dressed in a neatly embroidered outfit for the occasion, motioned them to get ready as they nervously looked discreetly at the host, *Emir* Moustafa El-Gandour, awaiting his permission to begin the entertainment.

When the musicians were finally granted permission to play their melodious rhythms, two rows of attractive belly dancers gracefully made their way through the tables to the center of the splendid hall. At first, the stunning women assembled in a circle with their backs to the spectators, then turned and cleverly dropped their transparent veils that covered their faces. Except for only a few trinkets and charms on their arms, their attractive bodies were fully exposed under unusually translucent colourful outfits. They began to dance alluringly and artfully, moving each part of their bodies to demand the attention of debating *Emirs* to help them alleviate their tensions.

Aromatic Turkish tobacco smoke fused with exotic feminine perfume evoked an atmosphere of true pleasure to a point of madness. Suddenly, the splendid hall was transformed into a frenzy of seduction and infinite eternal ecstasy.

12

According to countless hieroglyphic inscriptions and legends, the ancient Egyptian Pharaohs, in some way or another, believed that the body and the soul were two separate entities. They assumed that death was only a temporary separation of the soul from the body. They also alleged that if the body was well preserved, then the soul would someday be restored to it. Many hieroglyphic inscriptions on papyrus and on tablets were left next to tombs and sarcophagi containing spells and curses to assist in the process of re-uniting the soul with the preserved body. Mummification was a secret art performed only by ancient priests to preserve the corpse so that it would remain intact and ready for the spirit to rejoin it in the future.

*****

After a ride that lasted almost an hour, Mahroos and Carole saw in the distance a small village with several stone built homes and many primitive huts. On the outskirts of the village, they saw some children playing a kind of a war game. The amusement stopped and a few dogs barked as Mahroos, Carole, and the two boys approached a well to refill their jugs with fresh water. One of the children ran to a house to announce them as intruders while another older boy approached and asked what they wanted. Mahroos did not answer the youngster and continued to refill their containers with water. He then drank and helped Carole dismount her donkey. As instructed earlier by Mahroos, Carole's head was fully covered and only her eyes were visible. Holding a cane, an elderly man, followed by four other men, appeared from behind a building while three others approached slowly from another direction. Mahroos focused on the elder, then said, "Peace be upon you."

The white-bearded elder regarded Mahroos, Carole, the two donkey boys, and the donkeys. "Welcome to you all. Let's go over there in the shade. Where are you coming from and where are you headed, dear son?" He then pointed to a large primitive sunshade with sheepskin mats scattered under it. The two donkey boys held onto the harnesses of their donkeys and did not make a move while Mahroos and Carole followed the bearded old man who sat in the shade. Three of the men sat next to the elder facing Mahroos and Carole while the others and the children watched from nearby. Though it was not yet spring, the sun was warm and a slight breeze carried a fine film of sand over their faces. The old man touched his head cover and stared at Mahroos.

Mahroos adjusted his position, gathered his thoughts, and explained, "We thank you for receiving us so kindly. We came directly from Cairo and we're on our way to Dar-Abu-Arab. Our intention is simply to see what they have to offer there in terms of merchandise."

"This is Dar-Abu-Arab and I'm Abu-Arab himself. This is my home and my whole family. You're at the right place. You're then our guest and will have lunch with us."

"That is very generous of you, Sheik Abu-Arab, but unfortunately we have to decline your generous invitation. We have seven children waiting for us at home and we must return before sunset."

At this, Carole looked at Mahroos in surprise but immediately realized that he had to know what to do with such people. In a way, she was happy that he had introduced her as his fantasy wife and the mother of seven imaginary children. She was happy that her smile could not be seen from beneath her head cover.

"My name is Mahroos and I am a merchant from Cairo. Travellers from everywhere come to my establishment to shop for ancient artifacts. I truly don't see why anyone would pay good money for such objects but, in any case, that's what they require. My Upper Egypt supplier hasn't shown up for over a month and I'm running short of supplies. I was told that I might find what I need here and decided to come personally and have a look. If I find that your merchandise is suitable for my clients, then you might become my one and only supplier."

Though she remained silent as instructed, Carole could not believe how Mahroos could fabricate such a convincing story. She noticed Sheik Abu-Arab nodding in agreement with Mahroos. To her surprise, Abu-Arab motioned to one of the boys who stood nearby. The boy came running to the old man who whispered a few words in his ear. The boy ran again towards one of the buildings and returned with a small marble statue and gave it to Sheik Abu-Arab. Proudly, the old man looked at the statue, smiled, and then handed it to Mahroos.

"He made it. It's a replica of what we once found in a tomb. We had to mark the original because the two statues are so incredibly alike."

Mahroos exclaimed, "Unbelievable! Unbelievable! Where did you learn how to do such an artful intricate carving?" Mahroos asked the young boy.

"Here," the boy answered shyly as he took the statue to return it to its proper place.

"Would you like to come and see the workshop, to get an idea of what we offer? Your wife may join the harem and wait for us there if she wants."

"Yes, of course! I would like to see the shop, and with your permission, my wife will accompany us as well."

The old man led the way followed by Mahroos, Carole, and the three other men who were sitting with them. When they reached a stone built hall, one of the men opened the door and they all entered. The floor was tiled with granite and on the perimeter were hundreds of small statues of many sizes, shapes, and material. Mahroos browsed slowly, pretending to examine and admire the work. He stopped several times and carefully held one item or another while Carole followed in his footsteps.

"This is even much better than I had thought. I would certainly consider becoming your loyal client. In a few days, I'll come with some of my men to make a deal."

They returned to the shed and sat in the same places as before. Mahroos did not know yet how to raise the subject of the Mummies. Carole was still pondering the next moves as well.

"I'm very sorry that you can't join us for lunch but, before you depart, let's at least have coffee as a sign of friendship," invited the old man.

"We really must go now but, to tell you the truth, I can't turn down a second invitation. We'll just have coffee before we leave."

While the aroma of freshly-made coffee began to fill the air, Mahroos referred to some of the many items that he had seen and admired at the shop. He then casually asked, "Sheik Abu-Arab, you've mentioned tombs. Are there many tombs around here?"

"More than you can imagine. This region is loaded with tombs. It seems like the ancients buried all their dead here in one place."

"What do you normally find inside?"

"Well! Not much. Our hope is to find gold and we were lucky a couple of times. Not as much as we desired but every little bit helps. Usually, we find jars that contain some belongings of the deceased and, of course, the granite sarcophagi. They aren't easy to open but the hope of finding gold gives us the needed energy and strength to open them. Every now and then, we discover a piece of gold beside the Mummy."

Mahroos asked with surprise, "Mummy?"

"A Mummy is a kind of preserved body of a deceased person. Didn't you know that?"

"Oh yes! I know what you mean, Sheik Abu-Arab, I'm just curious. What do you do with them?"

"Well, practically nothing! Sometimes in the winter when we're short of wood, we burn them to cook and to keep ourselves warm. In fact, they burn much better and longer than wood."

"The reason I am interested is that recently one of my regular clients asked if I had Mummy fragments."

"You really mean that someone was willing to pay for pickled bodies?"

"As you know, merchants never say no to a client and I simply informed him that I may have delivery of some soon," Mahroos said while laughing aloud.

Curiously, the old man asked, "How much would he pay for that?"

"How much would you pay for a Mummy?" Mahroos asked in a jocular manner.

Coffee was now being served by a young boy wearing a long white shirt. From a metal pot, he carefully filled a cup for each and politely left.

"I pay nothing of course! But, let me make a suggestion for you. What if I give you a couple of sacks filled with Mummy fragments as a gift for a trial period? If your client shows up again, you would have the needed merchandise. In the future, if he asks for more, well, you know where to find me and we would then discuss prices. Is that fair?"

"That's quite fair and generous enough," Mahroos said smiling.

The old man motioned to one of the three men who perfectly understood what to do. In a short while, he returned with two sacks each containing Mummy fragments. Unhurried, Mahroos finished his coffee, thanked and embraced the old man, shook hands with the other three, and helped Carole mount her donkey. Slowly they rode towards the city. When they reached the city walls, it was Carole's turn to hold her stomach to manage her uncontrollable, unstoppable laughter.

"I know a coffee supplier in the city who has the facilities to crush your Mummies into powder. That way they would be even easier to store and transport in small sacks," Mahroos offered.

"Thanks, Mahroos. You are very kind," Carole replied smiling.

13

After the debate that took place hours earlier in the grand hall at *Emir* Moustafa El-Gandour's palace, disappointed Zafaran *Bey* was on his way home. Despite his persuasive speech and warnings regarding Mohammed Ali's deceptive character, it seemed quite clear that most of the leading *Emirs* of Cairo had accepted the invitation to the Citadel. He repeatedly asked himself: *How could they trust that swindler?* Though there were still a few days till Friday, even a glimpse of hope of reversing their decision to accept the Pasha's invitation was too optimistic. There was no doubt in his mind that the decision was final.

Absorbed in his thoughts, he dismounted his horse, handed the harness to a servant, and entered the house. He sat quietly and evaluated his own views. To join the Mamelukes would be unwise and yet not to accompany them would seem cowardly and spineless. He not only belonged to that elite of warriors but he was also a proud part of it.

Unexpectedly, his father-in-law walked in and sat on the large pillow opposite him. After a moment of silence, he slowly rubbed his grey beard and seemed pensive.

"What have you gentlemen decided? I guess they didn't listen to you. I should have gone myself and told them all what I thought about Mohammed Ali and I would have been able to convince them one by one, if needed."

Disappointed and depressed, Zafaran *Bey* finally bewailed, "Look, I tried my best but they think that they can outwit him once his army has left."

"They definitely can't con Mohammed Ali. Remember, you've two children and your wife is expecting a third!"

"Well, here's what we'll do as a precaution. I've already sent a messenger to my friend, Salama, to expect you and the family. Then, sometime tomorrow, you'll take Salwa and the children to visit him. I understand that it's a long and harsh way out in the western desert, but as you know, Upper Egypt is out of the question."

"That's exactly what I foresee. Do you think I should take some spare money with me?"

"It's always a good idea to take more than what you normally need. In any case, if you require anything else, I'm sure Salama would help. I know that it's still a few more days till Friday but we should start moving as of tomorrow."

"You're reading my mind," uttered his father-in-law.

Later, Zafaran *Bey* entered the bedroom and found his wife reclining on the bed. She stretched her arms towards him and he immediately bent and hugged her. He looked kindly at her delicate face and remembered when he had unveiled her the first time on their wedding night. He gently touched her pregnant belly and said, "It's going to be very soon. I can tell!"

She smiled and answered calmly, "Is it going to be here or somewhere else?"

"I'm afraid it has to be somewhere else. I made a strong case but I failed to convince the *Emirs*. They're so determined to accept the invitation. How stupid can they be? Anyway, my love, I've already decided with your father that he'll take you and the children to visit Salama's family. I can't think of a safer place."

"When are we leaving, my love?"

"It would certainly be better sooner than later. We've decided before noon tomorrow."

"I'm very much worried about you. All seems so unpredictable. Couldn't you just leave them and come with us? What shall we do without you?"

"You know very well that I can't do that. I'm a part of the whole and must go with them no matter what. There's nothing for you to worry about. I'll be safe, God willing! A messenger will ask Salama to send some of his men to keep an eye on you from afar. Just take care of yourself and the children."

The door suddenly opened and a sleepy Moniera, their daughter, walked into the room and dropped herself on the bed between them. As their daughter opened her eyes, she asked, "Am I going to have a brother or another sister?"

"Does it make any difference to you?" her father answered.

"I've told you many times, Moniera, that only God knows the answer to that question," responded her mother with a smile. Salwa hugged her daughter, drew her closer, and continued, "Now, go to sleep. We have a long journey ahead of us tomorrow. We'll visit your dear friend, Fawzeya, the daughter of Uncle Salama."

Moniera said, "That's really great. I'll sleep right away so that tomorrow comes sooner!"

That night, Zafaran *Bey* could not sleep. He sat by himself in the dimly-lit reception room thinking about the debate and its outcome. He wondered how so many *Emirs* could even consider trusting an Ottoman Pasha. Zafaran *Bey* remembered the history of the Mamelukes and mulled it over in his mind.

*****

The legend of the Mameluke rule in Egypt is quite amazing. Despite a strange and mysterious origin, their empire reigned for several centuries over Egypt and other parts of the region. Adapting a baronial system quite similar to what had been fairly common at the time in Europe, the Mamelukes freely controlled and governed the country. Yet the peculiar dilemma of their dynasty was that the Mamelukes were not only foreign to Egypt but that they were initially purchased as young boys by other Mamelukes.

Commonly, Mamelukes represented a mixture of East European and Asian origins. As young as ten years old, Mamelukes were either purchased or stolen from their parents by slave traders and then sold to a *Sultan, Emir* or *Bey*. The boys were expected to be strong, well-built, and handsome. Even though they were purchased, they became an integral part of the Mameluke system by their adoptive organization. Restricted to military barracks, they received rough and thorough training to become loyal soldiers to serve and protect their owners. With absolutely no connection to their origins or past, they respected their owners by showing complete devotion and appreciation of their military upbringing. Egypt was where they grew up and the country became their home. Once they had perfected their military skills, they were granted not only their freedom but also fiefs, other lands, and opportunities to rise in the ranks. Depending on their aptitude and capabilities, they could become *Beys, Emirs* or even Sultans. To maintain their power and authority when they reached such a high level, the Mamelukes continued the tradition of purchasing hundreds of young boys to be raised and trained as they had been. Amazingly, that cycle continued for centuries.

Literally, the Arabic word 'Mameluke' means *owned*. The word *maalek* means owner and yet the word *malek* also means 'king.' Interestingly, the word Mameluke in Arabic, of course, has a royal ring to it despite its literal meaning. Yet the Mamelukes lived and acted not just like kings but rather as superior beings. In their superb silky, colourful bright clothes, decorative jewellery, and weaponry, the Mamelukes projected a remarkable impression of pre-eminence. Though they recklessly and savagely fought among themselves, the Mamelukes were known to indulge in a luxurious lifestyle. They lived in elaborate palaces and built spectacular mosques; however, their contact with ordinary Egyptians was limited to tax collection, extortion, subjugation, and, occasionally, slaughter. Of foreign origin, the Mamelukes treated the native Egyptians as inferior. Very few Mamelukes married Egyptian women. Instead, the majority preferred Asian or East European females. According to their laws of inheritance, however, their offspring could not become heirs to their titles or positions.

Indeed, there had been countless avenues that led to the creation of a Mameluke dynasty in Egypt. The most remarkable one was the reign of Queen Shagaret-el-Dorr (Tree of Pearls). Unprecedented in an Islamic society, Shagaret-el-Dorr became the first Sultana or Queen to rule Egypt. Of unknown origin, Shagaret-el-Dorr was the slave of Sultan Saleh Ayyub of Egypt. In the culture and society of the time, it must be realized that being a purchased slave really meant becoming an adopted member of the family. Due to Shagaret-el-Dorr's extraordinary beauty and shrewdness, the Sultan fell in love and married her. The Sultan's death coincided with the seventh crusade's attempted invasion of Egypt by King Louis IX of France. Shagaret-el-Dorr kept her husband's death a secret and continued to rule the country and direct the leadership of the army. On their way to capture Cairo, the crusaders were defeated by the Egyptians. King Louis IX of France was captured and held in the city of Mansoura at the house of Ebn Lukeman. For eighty days, Queen Shagaret-el-Dorr ruled Egypt before many intrigues and assassinations forced her to abdicate and marry a second husband. Later, Shagaret-el-Dorr was brutally killed by the female slaves of her new husband's wife. Her remains were gathered by some kind people and buried in her own mausoleum located near the Citadel. As time went by, the power and structure of the Mameluke ruling class became the norm in Egypt.

*****

Zafaran *Bey* came out of his reverie and felt cold in the reception room. He must have dozed off a bit but he began to recognize the likelihood that he might never ever see his loved ones again. His wife's questions: *Couldn't you just leave them and come with us? What shall we do without you?* echoed in his mind and touched his inner soul. He went to his children's room and gazed at his two sleeping daughters and saw them as angels. His heart ached as he recalled his own childhood. Returning to the reception room, he sat once again and contemplated his past: *What sort of childhood had he had? Who were his parents and where could they be now? Had he any brothers or sisters?* These were the same questions that had always haunted him throughout his life. He could only manage to remember a few vague events from his past and yet, despite his urge to know, there had always been a strong, inner rejection of his past. As a young Mameluke, the only solace from his ancestry was what his old military trainer at the garrison had once told him: *What counts is the present not the past.* His old military trainer had repeatedly warned his regiments of the dangerous Ottomans and insisted vehemently on regarding them as the real enemies of all the Mamelukes. Finally, sleep once again overpowered his conflicting and disturbing thoughts as he gradually began to float into fantasy engendered by his own dreams.

At dawn, Salwa was up packing and preparing for the unexpected trip. She gathered what was needed in large sacks for an unforeseeable length of time. After sunrise, Salwa, her father, and the two children exited the city gate disguised as *fellaheen* (farmers). Discreetly, they were later met by Bedouin from Salama's tribe who helped and protected them. Fortunately, they were never stopped by Ottoman soldiers or highway robbers. The following day, they safely reached their destination at Salama's Bedouin encampment.

14

In the morning Mahroos noticed that, as usual, Seaham had left the room earlier. He gazed at the ceiling and thought of his little adventure with Carole the day before and that he had actually succeeded in fulfilling her request by obtaining Mummies perfectly compacted into powder. He touched his cheeks where she had kissed him last night while softly asking to see him again the following day. He knew that tomorrow he would join Zeyad Abu Ali to attend an evening celebration. The day after was set for his adventure with his old friend, Awaad. The only time he could see Carole was today, he thought. The fact that she herself had asked him to return made him even happier. While washing and dressing, he wondered why he wanted so eagerly to see her and speculated what she would ask of him this time.

In the distance, he spotted the two donkey boys waiting at the gate of Monsieur Dumont's home. He knew that they would be waiting as he had paid them generously yesterday. He was about to enter the courtyard while Monsieur Dumont and his wife were leaving. He greeted them politely and noticed that Carole was in the courtyard as well waiting in the same place as the day before.

Monsieur Dumont turned to Mahroos and inquired, "Did you enjoy Saqqara yesterday? Today is easier. Carol only wants to see a few Coptic churches in the city. You're very welcome to have supper with us, Mahroos."

Not wanting to mention a word about Saqqara, Mahroos replied, "No problem! I know where all the churches are and, if I can, I'll stay for supper. Thank you."

After Dumont and his wife left, Carole sat quietly on a bench in the courtyard. Mahroos went and sat at the other far end. For a while, they remained in complete silence.

"I was lucky to leave yesterday with two kisses on the cheek. This morning I don't even get a hello. Could that be one of the aftereffects of the Mummies on you?"

Carole remained silent and Mahroos continued, "Well, if I remember correctly, yesterday the destination was supposed to be Saqqara and yet we went to Dar-Abu-Arab. Today, the plan is to visit some churches which, in reality, mean what?"

"I want to visit Aleyya-Bent-Ali, the exorcist," Carole answered with an earnest frown.

Again, Mahroos held his stomach trying to manage his uncontainable laughter which he pretended to be a severe cough. The gate keeper rushed to him with a jug of water and patted him on the back. Mahroos drank some water, thanked the gate keeper, and sat again in full control of his emotions. Breathing hard but regularly, he eyed Carole and wondered what brought such an unusual idea into her head.

Carole replied, "Are you taking me there or shall I go back into the house?"

"Listen! I'm staying at a nice *kahn* not very far from here. What do you say we go there to my comfortable room and discuss your exorcism idea in private?"

Carole answered in a direct tone of voice, "Sounds like a great idea to me but I really want to discuss exorcism with

Aleyya-Bent-Ali and she lives in the Mokattam district. Do you want to help or not?"

Despite her distinct French accent, Mahroos admired Carole's knowledge of Arabic. He noticed that the gate keeper was watching them curiously so he deliberately lowered his voice.

"What I would like to know, first of all, is why on earth you are so rigid and passive towards me today? What have I done contrary to what you asked me to do? I find that the exorcism issue is just as bizarre as the Mummies, if not even more so. All I'm asking for is some explanation."

"My husband was an officer with Napoleon's army. He was killed during the invasion at the famous Battle of the Pyramids not very far from here. I believe that Aleyya-Bent-Ali, the exorcist, is capable of calling on his spirit."

"Calling on his spirit and then what?" Mahroos asked while seemingly the world was spinning under his feet.

"Well, then I would talk to him."

"Yes! Of course, talk to him, talk to him!"

Mahroos spoke quietly as they walked towards the gate. He then helped Carole mount the donkey and they rode at a slow pace to the Mokattam district.

When they reached the center of that district, Mahroos motioned to one of the donkey boys and asked him to inquire where Aleyya-Bent-Ali lived. To his surprise, the boy told him that he knew exactly where she lived as he, on many occasions, had brought other clients to her. The boy led them through several mazes of narrow lanes and constricted passageways that finally led to the dead end of a lane with a mysterious huge door. Snakes and other reptiles were artfully carved on the heavy wooden access. Mahroos used a black metallic ring that hung from the jaw of a carved lion to knock on the door. It took a few more knocks for the door to open narrowly. From behind, a tall slender woman appeared with tattoos on her forehead. Like Cleopatra, her eyes were outlined in unusually thick black lines. Wisps of grey hair peeked from her head cover suggesting a thick abundance of hair. In addition to large earrings, she wore a third ring on her nose and the appendage almost covered her lips. Although a shawl draped her shoulders, her large bosom revealed sensuous cleavage spilling over her silky bodice. She was an extremely attractive woman yet the energy emanating from her presence caused fright and panic in those facing her. While the two boys retreated and stood half-hidden behind their donkeys, Mahroos stepped forward and asked if he and Carole could enter. After a comprehensive examination of Carole, the woman opened the door wide enough for them to pass through a long dark candle-lit corridor. Carole and Mahroos reached an enormous room decorated by strange objects that Mahroos could not recognize. A large black fur carpet almost filled the room and huge pillows in varying shades of grey, white, and black hugged the perimeter. The woman sat leisurely on a low heavy wooden chair. Opposite her were six other low wooden benches. Mahroos and Carole sat down hesitantly faced her. A massive rectangular well-cut tree trunk served as a table between them. Seven large candles flickered on the table top. Beside each candle were trays laden with a variety of sweetmeats. The woman chose a date and invited Mahroos and Carole to join her. The three of them slowly chewed on their dates each eying the other curiously. By tradition, at a gathering, eating together conveys mutual trust and friendship. Aleyya-Bent-Ali removed her shawl and spread it over the back of her seat. She removed her head cover revealing long, thick hair then leaned over and fingered a second date.

"Welcome! Make yourselves at home and eat at your pleasure."

Two female servants entered with coffee and water, served the guests, and quietly left the room. Mahroos interrupted the silence realizing that he had to begin explaining the purpose of their visit. He took two dates, handed one to Carole then said, "We're honoured to be in your company and thank you for your generosity. We truly need your help on a serious and difficult issue that I can't explain but possibly my wife ...."

Aleyya-Bent-Ali interrupted, "Your wife? If you want my help then we should and must be true about everything we say to each other."

Stunned, Mahroos looked at Carole who was just as surprised as he was. They both realized that they were in the presence of an extraordinary woman who might have the power to see into their minds and souls. Mahroos was quite embarrassed and his face dropped as he stared at the floor.

"I sincerely apologize. This young lady ... wants to communicate with her late husband," Mahroos replied humbly.

"Well! I offer a lot of free services for the deprived and desperate but I require from those who can pay a donation for the poor and needy spiritualists who constantly work with me behind the scenes. I'll charge you a moderate sum of seven golden coins for this sitting. If you agree, then please place each coin next to a candle on that table in front of you."

Mahroos looked at Carole again, reached for his secret belt under his garment, and extracted a purse. He counted seven coins and quietly placed each next to a candle. He was about to ask a question when Aleyya-Bent-Ali addressed Carole.

"Your husband is here with us right now. I truly don't know where exactly but he is present. What's the lady's name?" Aleyya-Bent-Ali asked Mahroos.

"Her name is Carole," Mahroos replied in a trembling voice.

The exorcist demanded, "Carole, welcome your husband in your own language and please repeat it a couple of times."

While tears rolled down her cheeks, Carole repeated several times in French, "Welcome Dominique!"

After a period of silence, unexpectedly Carole jumped up in disbelief saying, "He spoke to me. It's him. He spoke to me!"

Frightened, Mahroos inquired, "What did he say?"

"I'm coming tonight," Carole responded as she walked out of the house.

Without a word, they rode all the way back to Monsieur Dumont's home. Once there, Carole dismounted her donkey and moved through the gate. The poor old gate keeper could not conceal his astonishment when he saw her in a seemingly sleep-walking state. Mahroos observed her until she disappeared inside the house. He then paid the donkey boys and asked one of them to return the following morning at the *kahn*. He wondered whether he had done the right thing by taking Carole to an exorcist like Aleyya-Bent-Ali. Admittedly, he was frightened himself as the effect on Carole had been enormous. He was determined to see Carole once more in the morning.

15

The following morning Seaham, as usual, had left the room earlier. When Mahroos awoke, he was still upset by the experience of the previous day. Images of Aleyya-Bent-Ali and her bizarre reception hall troubled his mind and he was determined to leave immediately to see Carole. As he was about to call one of the servants, Seaham walked in with two pots of hot water for his bath. In a soft and loving way, she kissed him and bent to fill the small tub with water. He grabbed her waist from behind and held her while kissing her bare back and shoulders. She turned slowly around and looked him in the eyes.

"Though I have known you only for a few days, last night I noticed that you were different," whispered Seaham. "What happened?"

"What do you mean by different?" Mahroos said in surprise.

"Well, you were in a kind of rage. Your passion was not as tender and your thoughts seemed somewhere else."

"Don't be so sensitive."

"No, Mahroos. If you don't want to see me, I won't bother you. Just let me know. Are you worried about your wife and family?"

"No, Seaham, it's neither you nor my family. It's just that what happened yesterday was so bizarre, I simply can't make any sense out of it."

Mahroos seemed resigned. As he sat in the tub, Seaham began to wash and massage him. Instead of becoming aroused, he turned towards her and uttered, "If I tell you, you probably won't believe it."

While continuing to rub his manhood in a gentle manner, Seaham answered, "You're a good man, Mahroos, and I trust you. I'll believe anything you say."

He smiled, touched and kissed her, then related the story about taking Carole to visit Aleyya-Bent-Ali. Seaham dropped the towel she was about to hand him, retreated a few steps, and held her breath.

"You didn't go there with your friend's sister, did you?" asked Seaham.

"I did," Mahroos replied in sorrow and anguish.

"All I can tell you from the many people I know who visited her is that the Devil, demons, and all evil spirits reside with her. Any spirit she brings forth will permanently haunt the one in question."

"You mean that the spirit of Carole's husband will haunt her forever?"

"Yes, Mahroos, that woman will be haunted forever unless one or both of you go to Aleyya-Bent-Ali and reverse the request before noon today."

"Before noon today!"

"Yes, before noon. Timing is crucial, believe me!"

In no time and as never before, Mahroos was dressed and out of the *kahn*, telling Seaham that he would be back on time to honour the invitation with his friend, Zeyad Abu Ali. As expected, the donkey boy was waiting for him and they galloped to Aleyya-Bent-Ali. Distressed and frightened, Mahroos knocked at the heavy gate using the lion's ring. After being ushered in, he sat at the same place he had occupied the day before.

The rectangular heavy low table bore the same seven large lighted candles as well as the layers of sweetmeats. Again, Aleyya-Bent-Ali took a date and invited Mahroos to do the same. Hesitantly, he took one date and exclaimed, "I want to reverse the request we made yesterday."

Aleyya-Bent-Ali waited a few minutes before saying, "Where are the donations?"

Again, Mahroos reached for his secret belt under his garment and extracted a purse. He counted seven coins and quietly placed each next to a candle.

"To reverse a request that had been already fulfilled will cost double the donation!" Aleyya-Bent-Ali replied.

Mahroos almost jumped up and was about to object in protest but realized that he was facing a powerful and unpredictable entity. He counted another seven coins, placing each next to the others. A slight breeze suddenly blew from seemingly nowhere and swept over the candlelight. The room turned dark and the smell of burning wax filled Mahroos' nostrils.

"Is it done?" Mahroos asked.

"Yes, it is."

A huge male servant approached with a large candle to help Mahroos exit the house.

It was almost noon when Mahroos arrived at Monsieur Dumont's home. Carole, her brother, and Hameeda were seated in the reception hall as Mahroos entered.

Carole smiled at Mahroos and said, "Welcome! I thought you couldn't make it today."

"I'm really busy today, but decided to come and see how you were."

When Mahroos and Carole were alone, she whispered in his ear, "My husband was with me all night and even this morning. Just a short while ago, he strangely has vanished. I hope that he will return."

Mahroos had never before believed in spirits or exorcism; however, the clear visible changes in Carole's behaviour and expressions were enough grounds for him to reconsider.

16

Among his fellow Mameluke *Beys*, Nassar Kamel, the host, was known for his intense enthusiasm for acquiring, breeding, and arrogantly riding the finest of Arabian horses. How many horses he owned, no one really knew, yet almost everyone recognized that his collection was unrivalled. Although his many blonde Georgian concubines were undeniably his passion, horses, however, came to be an obsession. Nassar Kamel was indeed a proud member of *Emir* Moustafa El-Gandour's elite cavalry regiment and also one of his closest confidants. He was thrilled to know that he would ride among the first row of the Mameluke cavalry to follow *Emir* Moustafa El-Gandour in their procession to the Citadel. Delightedly, he ordered a feast to be held the night before the parade. Friends and friends of friends were welcomed. He hired and generously paid the best groups of entertainers, musicians, and dancers to perform. He had also engaged the finest caterers in Cairo to provide the most sumptuous food and sherbet drinks available. Welcoming staff and servants greeted and served the guests as they arrived and the palace seemed to hum in no time like a beehive.

When Zeyad Abu Ali, the *kahn* owner, and his friend, Mahroos, entered the palace, they were first given a special tour of the stables to see and admire the magnificent horses. A footman led them around unwillingly as he realized that they were ordinary Egyptians. He then ushered them into a hall where most guests were Mamelukes and told them in a polite tone to remain at the back. Unlike Zeyad, Mahroos felt uncomfortable among Mamelukes.

"What are we doing here surrounded by Mamelukes? I find it bizarre! Let us go to Awaad's coffeehouse where I'll feel more like myself."

"What horrible taste you've got? You prefer Awaad's dump over this elegance! What's the matter with you, my friend?"

"We're among Mamelukes. That's the matter."

A little further away from the crowd, they found a place to sit and observe all the other guests.

"Don't worry! Despite being a great Mameluke, Nassar Kamel considers me as a brother. You see, I once had the opportunity to save his life from a group of Ottoman soldiers. They were chasing him near my *kahn*. I provided him with shelter and protected him. The soldiers questioned and threatened to torture me but I refused to give in. For three days and several nights my *kahn* was under surveillance by spies. Only after almost a week did he feel safe to leave. A few weeks later, he came back to thank me. He gave me Seaham, the hostess you've met, and a purse full of gold as 'thank you' gifts."

"That's an unimaginable story," Mahroos replied. He then added, "I wish I could save his life ten times so I may get ten women like Seaham."

"Mahroos, you're the true devil himself when it comes to women!"

A shiny copper tray loaded with delicious food was placed in front of them. At the other end of the hall, they could see beautiful dancers moving seductively to the sound of music.

"Funny and outlandish at the same time," Zeyad offered while chewing happily on a chunk of meat. "Imagine! The soldiers almost killed him a few months ago. Now, he is celebrating to go into their burrow. Isn't that crazy?"

"I've heard that Mohammed Ali Pasha has recently ended hostility towards the Mamelukes and many of them live peacefully in Cairo. Is that true?"

"That may be true on the surface," affirmed Zeyad, "but underneath it all, the Pasha and his Albanian soldiers hate the Mamelukes."

"And the Mamelukes obviously hate them in return."

"Sometimes I feel that one day, they'll wipe each other out and we'll live happily ever after."

Nassar Kamel *Bey* suddenly appeared and greeted Zeyad. "Welcome, my dear brother. I hope that you're enjoying yourself. I didn't see you when you arrived. Was my palace hard to find?"

"No! Certainly not! This is my dear friend, Mahroos, who is visiting for a couple of weeks."

They shook hands. Nassar Kamel *Bey* then jokingly said, "I know that the *kahn* is quite comfortable and pleasant but if you find it otherwise, I have a lot of space here."

The music stopped. Dancers ran timidly to a nearby wall and remained motionless. The crowded hall became quiet. Nassar Kamel, the host, stood in the middle of the throng and gazed at his guests in a welcoming manner. He raised his right arm and loudly bellowed, "Dear brothers and guests, I welcome you! Please, consider this your home. You're all at home here!"

A loud applause of gratitude echoed from all corners of the majestic hall. Nassar Kamel raised his right arm again and continued, "Tonight we celebrate tomorrow. Yes, brothers, tonight we celebrate tomorrow because tomorrow I'll be riding right behind our great leader, *Emir* Moustafa El-Gandour. Yes, riding to enter the Citadel, our Citadel. The Pasha of Egypt is now living in our Citadel which was built by the most extraordinary man of all men, Saladin. I'll be proud to be inside that Citadel."

After the long repetitive speech had ended, Mahroos still felt uncomfortable.

"I hope that they don't collide tomorrow with the Ottoman soldiers. But whom do you think would decisively win if they were to fight a war?"

"Unfortunately, all the Mamelukes still bask in their old glories. Nothing new was learned from fighting the French. Despite their enormous courage, they've never comprehended that riding a horse while cleverly swinging a sword is a thing of the past. Sadly, they'll never comprehend it."

Amazed by such an analysis, Mahroos uttered, "Let them both eat each other alive. I've had enough of both Turks and Mamelukes."

Musicians and the many dancers returned to their joyful performances while servants distributed trays loaded with delicacies. Awhile later, Mahroos remembered his meeting the following day.

"I need to see Awaad tomorrow morning before the Friday prayers. Can I just walk out and leave?"

"Of course, you can leave! No one here will miss you; however, if you wait a few more moments, we can enjoy watching my favourite dancer. I promise to leave with you right after."

17

At dawn, the melodious call to first prayer reached Zamarawy's ears while he snored loudly in his exceptionally large bed. Fully naked, laying on his back with both arms stretched at his sides and his mouth wide open, he frequently wheezed for air changing the cadence of his breathing. He was almost at the end of his recurring, terrifying dream: *Falling off a cliff then intercepted by the huge jaws of a lion,* so began the dream, *the ferocious lion reconsiders eating him and with a disgusting roar ejects him over another cliff. The terror begins when he lands in a lake to be torn apart into countless chunks and chewed by dreadfully hungry crocodiles.*

Out of breath, Zamarawy released a harsh, loud cry that almost shook the entire house. As usual, he jumped off his bed and touched nearly every part of his massive body to reassure himself that he was still in one piece. He heard knocking at the door as he was about to plunge back into bed. Polite calls from his two Abyssinian concubine girls for permission to enter reached his ears. Immediately, he remembered his commander's orders to be at the Citadel before sunrise. He thanked God for telling the girls about his early appointment the night before. He stretched his immense arms and legs then shouted, "Come in you two bitches and wash me fast. How come you're so late?" he roughly added.

Each carrying two jugs of hot water, the Abyssinian girls entered the room. Both were covered only with white gowns and seemed like identical twins. Their tall erect bodies along with their pointed well-formed breasts revealed the splendour of youth and beauty. Like a ritual, the moment they emptied the jugs into a small metallic tub at the far end of the room, they dropped their gowns. Dim light from a small oil lamp glistened exposing the softness and perfection of their skin. Their delicate faces radiated a magical charm. Like legendary goddesses, each girl stood motionless in an unspoken promise of passion, projecting a unique conceptual fervour for love. Their exquisite lips parted and turned into nervous smiles while waiting for the officer to fondle them. Yet, all went unnoticed by the Albanian high-ranking officer who simply jumped carelessly into the tub. One girl washed and soaped him while the other massaged his hairy body. Using both his hands, Zamarawy manhandled the girls' bodies as though they were animals. The girls continued their task submissively, knowing that in a few minutes their horror would soon end.

It was still dark when Zamarawy mounted his horse followed by six guards who had been awaiting him outside his house. While on his way to the Citadel, he unhappily remembered his horrific dream. He resisted the urge to touch his neck and the rest of his body for reassurance that he was still alive. Changing his thoughts, he wondered why four units of two hundred and fifty men each should be at the Citadel that early. His confusion was worsened by questioning the whole idea of a parade. Such extraordinary preparation for a parade did not make any sense. He found that the street decorations were excessive.

The free food stalls were not only enormous but also plentiful. The atmosphere, in general, was unreasonable considering the occasion. His genuine loyalty to Mohammed Ali Pasha was indisputable yet he could not comprehend the Pasha's decision to send an army under the command of his seventeen year old son, Tousoun, to fight in Arabia. It was not only the war against the Wahhabis in Arabia that troubled Zamarawy but also the severity of the hot climate and the remote territories of an unusually arid desert. In fact, he thought that it was not an occasion to rejoice but rather a time for advanced grieving.

The Bab Al-Azab gate to the Citadel was already open and people were beginning to gather at the square in front. Followed by his guards, Zamarawy passed through the gates and rode up the steep narrow passage leading to the army headquarters. His regiment of two hundred and fifty Albanian soldiers was waiting along with three others in the courtyard. Their commanding officers, who equalled Zamarawy in rank, stood at ease nearby. He greeted them and then asked, "Can anyone make sense of all this?"

"The General will soon be here ...."

One of the officers started to respond but suddenly stopped as a guard approached and led them into the General's office.

"Good morning, gentlemen. Please remain at ease."

The General spoke in a rough commanding tone. His huge moustache covered his upper lip and part of his cheeks.

"As of now, my orders are quite simple. All your regiments must remain armed, ready and concealed on top of the high walls over the passage leading to the Bab Al-Azab gate. I stress again the word 'concealed.' Obviously, many questions may be going through your heads about what may happen and what our objectives are. Honestly, for now, these are my orders. They come directly from the Pasha himself." He then pointed at Zamarawy and another officer and said, "You two, take the east and west lower sides of the walls near the gates. The others will take the two upper sides."

"Could it be that the Arabians are making a move on Cairo?" inquired an officer.

"There is no room for speculation! Understood? Follow your orders and make sure that your men bear their muskets with sufficient ammunition. Expect the unexpected. Understood?"

With these words, the General ended the meeting. On their way out to the courtyard, the officers were baffled and surprised.

"Orders are coming directly from the Pasha himself," shouted an officer.

Another added, "Could the Wahhabis be already in Cairo? What do you think?"

Zamarawy shook his head and stated, "They don't even know that the young Tousoun will be parading his way through Cairo in celebration of going to war against them. We're in complete darkness here and confront absolute ambiguity."

"Our salaries were paid in full yesterday including all old outstanding balances. The soldiers are very happy about it. I don't really care what may happen today," confided an officer as he walked towards his regiment.

The sun was about to rise when Zamarawy ordered his deputies to lead the soldiers to the eastern lower end of the Citadel wall near the Bab Al-Azab gate. Due to the height of the walls, it was naturally impossible for anyone entering or leaving the gates to see any of the soldiers who were above. Yet Zamarawy stressed the concealment orders to his deputies just the same.

On top of both walls that overlooked the narrow, steep passage leading up to the height of the magnificent historic Citadel, a little over a thousand armed men waited with their weapons ready.

18

In an extravagantly festive mood, the eternal city of Cairo welcomed a new day. Like never before for a long time, people wondered how it all had happened overnight. Streets were exceptionally clean, Ottoman flags were mounted everywhere, and huge inviting food stalls were serving the poor and everyone else a delicious breakfast. Preparations for lunch and supper were already underway. Small bands of musicians and dancers were gathered at every corner. Joy and laughter could be seen and heard by all. Though they all knew that it was a celebration of Mohammed Ali's son's departure to Arabia to fight a war, no one had ever thought that it would be such an elaborate and impressive occasion. People were stunned to see the amount of food that was being transported to the Citadel for the grand entertainment. Never before had the people of Cairo ever seen so many cooks, servants, and butlers dressed in their finest garments, heading towards the Citadel. People were proud to see their legendary city sparkle, exposing its beauty, generosity, and peacefulness. Religious dignitaries, merchants, workers, water-carriers, women and children, and even beggars were exhilarated by some magical delightful spirit.

Though his tiny store was no more than a few feet in width and depth, it housed a baffling number of shelves and drawers in a variety of sizes. Yet Sheik Mukrum El Attar, the owner, knew where everything was. As *attar* or chemist, he knew all about herbs, minerals, and many of the valuable extracts from plants and animals as well as insects. Sheik Mukrum El Attar was one of the best if not the best chemist in Cairo. From as far as Alexandria in the north to Aswan in the south, people came to him seeking remedies for all kinds of different ailments. Owing to his superior knowledge, honesty, and integrity, he was highly respected and appreciated by all his faithful clients. On occasion, his good friend, Sheik Ashraf, would come to spend some time with him especially in the morning. He had always welcomed such a visit as it gave him some diversion and kept him up-to-date with what went on in the neighborhood. Usually, they would order coffee and two water-pipes from the nearby coffeehouse.

Early morning, Sheik Mukrum *El Attar* sat in front of his tiny store wondering as everyone else why such an extravagant displays to celebrate the occasion of a war. Shaking his head in astonishment and disbelief, he noticed his friend, Sheik Ashraf, approaching, followed by two waiters from a nearby coffeehouse. One waiter carried two water-pipes and the other carefully held a copper tray with two small pots filled with freshly made Turkish aromatic coffee.

"You are just as decadent and wasteful as they are!" said Sheik Mukrum laughingly to his old friend.

"You haven't seen it all yet. This is only the tobacco and coffee. A dozen dancing girls are on their way," replied Sheik Ashraf jokingly.

The two old friends sat in silence for a while as one of the two waiters served coffee and the other filled the water-pipes with tobacco and glowing charcoal and made sure that the smoke flowed perfectly even at the slightest drag. Sheik Ashraf gave each waiter a generous tip and asked them to return later for a refill.

After he blew an enormous cloud of smoke, marking his first tobacco fix of the day, followed by a slurp of coffee, Sheik Ashraf finally leaned over and uttered to his friend, "I wonder what the excitement is about. The Pasha's young son and his army are about to engage in a dangerous war."

Nothing came in response from his friend, Sheik Mukrum *El Attar*, who squinted his eyes in an attempt to focus on a few dancing girls performing across the street.

"Have you seen how many roasted lambs and turkeys were transported to the Citadel? In my estimation, they had enough to feed the entire city and a whole army for a couple of days," Ashraf replied in an amazed tone.

"That's only what you've seen. Imagine all the stuff they've been shipping all week," Mukrum *El Attar* answered, after turning his face towards his friend, "All *Emirs* and many of their Mamelukes are invited. Don't you find it odd after so many years of skirmishes and fighting?"

"Yes, I find it peculiar too but maybe he wants the Mamelukes to join the fight in Arabia."

"Mamelukes will never fight a Sultan's war. My guess is that Mohammed Ali wants them to be on his side at least until the war ends ."

"That is definitely a clever idea."

A Bedouin arrived on a camel, greeted Sheik Mukrum *El Attar*, and then allowed the camel to descend and fold down his four legs. The Bedouin jumped gracefully off the hump and pulled out a small sack from a large woollen bag and placed it on the tiny counter in Sheik Mukrum *El Attar's* store. Despite Sheik Mukrum *El Attar's* insistence on paying for the delivery and offering coffee, the Bedouin declined to take any money declaring that he might do so next time. As the Bedouin was about to mount his camel, he noticed a large unit of Mameluke cavalry coming in his direction. He waited patiently until they all passed then swiftly mounted his camel. Immediately, the camel was on his front knees, then the rear legs were fully erected, and in seconds, the beast stood on all fours. The Bedouin bid his *Salam* and slowly vanished into the swarming crowd.

A while later, a young girl accompanied by four women slowly approached *El Attar's* shop. Sheik Mukrum interrupted his smoking and went to greet them while his friend Sheik Ashraf observed the four veiled females attentively. Each of the four had her own way of explaining and describing the symptoms of whatever ailed the young girl as Sheik Mukrum *El Attar* carefully listened to each of them. He then went into his shop and from one of the many tiny drawers, he scooped out at least eight spoons of some kind of a powder into a small pot. He gave the remedy, along with some verbal instructions, to one of the women whom he assumed to be the mother.

"Women keep you busy, my dear friend!"

While pointing to the large number of proud cavalry, he exclaimed in surprise, "Look! Look over there! Hundreds of the Mamelukes are heading towards the Citadel."

"I'm sure that they all know how to eat well. I hope that the host has enough food to fill all their bellies," Sheik Mukrum *El Attar* responded with a grin.

Calls to Friday prayers clearly echoed throughout the city. Mosques soon were filled by devotees and worshippers. For about an hour or so, the city was tranquil and serene for the prayers. Then the celebrations and festivities resumed in full swing

19

With carefully measured footsteps, Mahroos walked through Cairo's cheerful throng heading towards Awaad's old establishment. As instructed, he had a long rope around his waist and wore wide baggy trousers under his long, oversized local shirt or *galabeia*. He had never seen so many happy people, so much food, so many musicians, dancers, and countless arrogant Mamelukes riding towards the Citadel. Suddenly, it hit him! He understood Awaad's choice of the day to remove the loot. Mamelukes, their guards, and servants were all on their way to the Citadel and, clearly, there would be less security at their palaces, if any at all. He then concluded that his friend, Awaad, was the smartest guy he had ever met. He smiled and almost began to dance with the joyful crowd. Shortly before he reached the establishment, a young woman gazed at him through her scant veil. Surely, he fully understood all that she was proposing through her striking black eyes. Yet, he knew very well that Awaad would never forgive him or even tolerate a minute of delay. Disappointed at a lost opportunity, he kept walking and happily concentrated on the fact that in a few hours his exceptionally large pockets would be fully loaded with Mameluke gold. On his arrival, two donkey boys and their beasts waited by the door of the shop. Only a few elderly patrons were present and Awaad sat at his usual place smoking. Without a word, Mahroos entered and sat next to him.

"The two boys out there will take us through back alleys to an abandoned palace not far from the one we're about to hit. From the back, we can use its vast, neglected gardens to reach our destination. Once there, I'll use my rope and a hook to reach and scramble up onto one of the balconies. You hide in the bushes and wait until I signal to you from the fourth window to the left of the balcony I mounted. That is when you come ready with your rope, and throw it high up so that I can pull you to join me. Once we're both up there, the treasure is ours."

Attentively, Mahroos listened without uttering a word. Somehow, he imagined that nothing could be that simple. Despite his faith and trust in Awaad's planning, serious doubts began to haunt him. He wished that he was back with his wife and children rather than in this smoky dim place. In fact, he asked himself why he was here anyway as he really did not need any more gold to live comfortably.

"Here! Take this," Awaad demanded while offering him a musket. "Only use it if it comes to a matter of life or death. It's loaded!"

"But I've never used one before," replied Mahroos in a shaky voice.

"All you've got to do is point and pull this trigger. What's so hard about that?"

"But surely that was not a part of the deal I agreed to. Remember!" Mahroos whispered.

"Very well, I'll keep both of them on me."

"When do we leave then?"

"We'll be on our way shortly after Friday prayers."

Awaad handed the two donkey boys a sack full of food and they all went on their way. When they finally reached the abandoned palace, Awaad ordered the boys to sit and eat their lunch and wait. Awaad and Mahroos treaded carefully through the abandoned palace.

All went as planned. When Mahroos stood next to Awaad behind the fourth window, they congratulated each other. They both knew they were in the room that housed the treasure. They stood motionless for a moment fearing that someone might come. To their surprise, only the sound of music, singing, and laughter echoed from the streets of Cairo. The celebration seemed to have reached a high peak. Awaad uttered in disbelief, "I've never seen or heard so many joyful people in my life. The Pasha's son should go to war every day."

Awaad moved slowly towards the three swords on the wall while Mahroos carefully followed in his footsteps. As Awaad was about to pull down the third sword handle, he said with a smile on his face, "Even the owner of this palace doesn't know anything of what you're about to see, my dear friend."

The sword handle was pulled, the wall moved and from behind, the gold sparkled, sending tremors through Mahroos' body.

"An amazing and delightful sight, isn't it, Mahroos? Have you ever imagined that such a thing could exist? "

Puzzled, Mahroos said, "How did you do that? And what are we going to do now?"

"What we're going to do now? Take all we can, my friend. Take all we can!"

As if possessed by the devil, they began filling their long trouser pockets with anything they could lay their hands on. While Awaad was reaching for a higher shelf, he froze for a moment, and then whispered, "God is great! Look at that!"

It was another sword handle similar to the one in the outside room. His mind started to race and he realized that it may be another handle that operates from the inside as well.

"Mahroos," Awaad whisperingly inquired, "would you do me a favour?"

"I know what you want. You want me to bring you a few camels to help you transport it all."

"No. I want you to go out and lock me in by using the sword handle that I pulled down earlier on the outside."

Mahroos, who was intensely preoccupied with the jewels, answered, "What would that do, open another door?"

"Please! Do as I say now, please!"

Laden with artifacts, Mahroos walked out with difficulty and checked, "Are you sure?"

"Yes, I'm sure. But don't pull it a second time unless you hear me knocking and screaming from in here."

The moment Mahroos pulled the sword handle, the door to the treasure room shut as expected. He waited a little then the door reopened. At once, they both realized that the mechanism, whatever it was, worked perfectly from either side. They smiled and continued to load their pockets. Despite their concentration on the loot, they suddenly halted and stared at one another. Each seemed to know what the other was about to say. Finally, Mahroos broke the silence in puzzlement, "What happened to the crowd out there? I no longer hear music or chanting. Could it be that they've served more food and they're busy eating again?"

"What I can distinctly and unmistakably hear now are many, many shots being fired. I wonder what's happening out there and who is shooting what?" stated a bewildered Awaad.

20

Throughout history, Egyptians have relentlessly recorded their epochs by erecting splendid buildings and monuments that dazzled the world. Most certainly, the Citadel of Saladin on top of the Mokattam Hill near Cairo rises as a colossal testimony to medieval design. To some, the Citadel was meant to be a palace that included military barracks. Others believed that the Citadel was intended to be the midpoint of a wall to protect Cairo from invaders. Whatever the intentions might have been, construction of the Citadel started and was only completed after Saladin's death. Al Malek El Kamel was the first ruler to declare the Citadel as his residence and also the headquarters of the Egyptian government. For almost seven centuries thereafter, the Citadel remained the center of authority in Egypt. In fact, the sight of the Citadel had always signified great power and commanded the utmost reverence.

The Bab Al-Azab gate, an enormous gigantic wooden door protected by two elevated massive towers, was the main access to the Citadel. A wide opening between the supporting structures, which connects the two rooms at the top of each tower, was used to pour boiling oil on enemies to deter them from entering. The colossal wooden door led to a steep, narrow passage enclosed by high solid walls. At the gate, the passage was considerably narrow for a handful of horse riders to enter at the same time. It then expanded gradually upward leading to an enormously vast courtyard. The steepness and pavement of the slope prevented even the most experienced cavalry from moving upwardly at a considerable pace. Once inside that passage, an overwhelming sense of entrapment and helplessness would prevail. Only upon reaching the open and vast courtyard at the top could one then experience a sense of freedom and relief.

*****

It was Friday morning, the first day of March 1811 when elegantly dressed Mameluke *Emirs* rode their finest Arabian horses towards the Citadel. Hundreds of them had accepted Mohammed Ali's invitation to join the celebration. Gold and expensive stones decorated their clothes, swords, and saddles. Arrogantly and bejewelled beyond imagination, they gracefully rode their magnificent horses among the cheering crowds towards the square near the Bab Al-Azab gate leading to the Citadel. Occasionally, they stopped to admire and praise one another. They saw themselves as supreme beings and truly believed that they deserved everything they possessed. On both sides, crowds cheered, waved, and greeted them. Some sprinkled rosewater in the air; others, believers in superstition, tossed crystals of salt as a protection from the evil eye. In return, the Mamelukes sprinkled coins of low value on the masses. This kind of interaction was unusual and the Mamelukes felt even more jubilant.

Facing the Bab Al-Azab gate, the *Emirs* and Mamelukes assembled smugly and were in complete readiness at Roumaliya Square. They were awaiting a ceremonial fanfare and a special drumbeat customary for the reception of Kings and Sultans. At the gate, a high ranking Ottoman general and a battalion of his officers saluted the leading *Emir* with the utmost honour. With similar respect, the leading *Emir* returned the salute and rode conceitedly towards the open Bab Al-Azab gate.

Only a few riding Mamelukes could enter the Bab Al-Azab gate at a time. Climbing the slope was not an easy task for either the horses or for the riders. Therefore, it took a few hours for the hundreds of *Emirs* and Mamelukes to reach and assemble again in an orderly fashion in the open courtyard at the top. The immense space at the summit resembled a huge gallery overlooking the city. A light cool breeze drifted on their faces and they were all happy to be out of that steep passage. They could see and hear the cheering crowd and the sound of military bands and local musicians. Ottoman flags fluttered all around the protective boundary of the courtyard and the atmosphere appeared peaceful and gracious. The four leading *Emirs* were assisted off their horses and led honourably into the reception hall to meet with Mohammed Ali Pasha while all the other Mamelukes waited in the courtyard outside.

When Zafaran *Bey* reached the open courtyard at the end of the passage, he felt a sense of relief. Contrary to his distrustful nature, he somehow was reassured and dismounted his horse. He peered through the door leading to the elegant reception hall and admired the stylish interior. Never before had he expected to see such elegance at the Citadel. He noticed the four leading *Emirs* as they waited for the Pasha to arrive. The sky above him was intensely blue and he walked alone to the far end of the enormous courtyard to its protective edge. The entire city below him appeared as a miniature model. The view amazed him and, at that moment, he appreciated life and everything around him. He gazed at his horse's eyes and wondered what that superb beast was actually thinking. Zafaran *Bey*'s thoughts were interrupted as he noticed that the Pasha had arrived and was warmly embracing and greeting his guests, the four leading *Emirs*. Coffee was served and what seemed like a friendly discussion began among them. At times, Mohammed Ali, who could only speak Albanian and Turkish, used his interpreter. Again, Zafaran *Bey*'s gaze returned to his horse and he patted the beast's long neck. The horse shook his upper torso back and forth as if it were pointing at the reception door. Zafaran *Bey* looked back into the hall and, to his full surprise, noticed that the Pasha had taken his leave with an apparent strange expression on his face. Zafaran *Bey* carefully observed the four *Emirs* as they leisurely and comfortably sat and waited for the Pasha's return. At the same time, he noticed that a contingent of ceremonial Albanian soldiers stood in formation at a distance from the passage leading down to the gate.

An hour later, the Pasha had not returned. When Zafaran *Bey* realized that the four *Emirs* had decided to leave the reception hall and actually walk out to their horses, his instinctive suspicions increased. The fact that the Pasha had not returned to accompany them or even say farewell to his guests was an intolerable act by any code of behaviour. At that moment, Zafaran *Bey* was convinced beyond any doubt that all his distrust of the Pasha was valid. Though he did not know what to make of the hundreds of Mamelukes waiting to leave and follow the four *Emirs* as well, his confused mind raced in all directions.

Disillusioned and bewildered, the four prominent *Emirs* led all the Mamelukes in attendance down the steep passage towards the gate. In front of them, guiding the way, marched the ceremonial contingent of Albanian soldiers.

On his horse, Zafaran *Bey* remained unnoticed at the rear end along with a handful of other suspicious Mamelukes. Intentionally missing his position in the second row, he eyed the protective railing edge of the courtyard and the fluttering flags. As time slowly went by, and most of the Mamelukes were on their way down to the exit, Zafaran *Bey* suddenly heard loud orders to close the gate. At the same time, another group of armed Albanian soldiers appeared and marched behind the unsuspecting Mamelukes heading down to the gate.

It was the alarm of all alarms to Zafaran *Bey* who instinctively jumped on his horse and raced in exactly the opposite direction towards the flags at the edge of the courtyard's protective edge. He looked at the ground below and felt being up in the heavens while earth seemed at an infinite distance beneath. A number of the armed Albanian soldiers pointed their guns at him and the few other Mamelukes near him. In a matter of seconds, two Mameluke heads were savagely blown up, spilling blood everywhere. The other remaining Mamelukes received several shots and they, too, fell off their horses. Still alive and on his horse, Zafaran *Bey*, at this very moment, had no other options left open to him except one. He leapt off the protective barrier!

21

Riding among hundreds of chief *Emirs* and Mamelukes, *Emir* Moustafa El-Gandour carefully descended the narrow passage leading to the exit of the Bab Al-Azab gate. Their visit with the Pasha had ended strangely. They were expected to leave the Citadel to join some procession in the city. El-Gandour's Arabian white horse was unusually troubled by the uneven, jagged, narrow passage which was badly carved into the rock of the Mokattam Hill. All the other *Emirs* had similar difficulties and their beasts were somehow reticent to move about. A group of ceremonial Albanian cavalry led the way ahead of the *Emirs* and Mamelukes. The presence of the Albanian cavalry was not unusual, yet it certainly was resented by all Mamelukes. They always considered them to be uncivilized hooligans.

It was a bright sunny day as they descended the narrow passage. The walls on both sides became higher and higher while a sense of murkiness and entrapment prevailed. Despite the different shouts and loud laughter by some of the Mamelukes at times, concern was written on many faces especially those of *Emir* Moustafa El-Gandour and his entourage. Contrary to the courteous and grand welcome they had received upon their arrival, their departure was peculiar and disappointing. Their hasty exit was due to the unexpected and abrupt disappearance of their host, Mohammed Ali. How could a leader simply leave his invitees after such an elaborate reception? That was the question that troubled most of the *Emirs*. They could not comprehend his sudden, mysterious departure. Soon enough, speculation about Mohammed Ali's desertion circulated. Some thought that he had gone to the *harem*, his women's quarters, while others claimed that it was due to a distress caused by his son's departure to fight in Arabia. With a man as demanding as Mohammed Ali, anything was possible. He could be everywhere and nowhere at the same time. Shrewdness and deception were the main ingredients of his personality.

Accidentally, *Emir* Moustafa El-Gandour's horse brushed with another and the neighbouring *Emir* exclaimed, "We're only halfway to the main gate. I wish this damn passage were wider and shorter."

Emir El-Gandour peered at the colossal limestone walls on both sides and marvelled at their craftsmanship and perfection. Behind him, he saw a sea of perfectly assembled cavalry of *Emirs* and Mamelukes in their best attire, with swords and arms at their sides. Puzzling questions crossed his mind once more: *What was the invitation really about? Why such a glamorous reception and such a sordid departure? What was in it for us to participate in a procession for a war that we have nothing to do with?* He could not find any satisfactory answers. He then turned towards the *Emir* next to him and shouted, "I'm with you! I can't wait to be out of here. Problem is, we're only halfway and can't ride any faster."

"We're not even told which part of the procession we'll be in. I hope that we don't follow his young son, Tousoun."

"I suppose, once we're out of here, the master of the ceremonial procession will tell us," El-Gandour remarked.

"What I really don't get is, we all go all the way up and then only a handful of *Emirs* see Mohammed Ali for a short while. Then we all come down again through this ragged passage. Honestly, Moustafa, does that make any sense to you?"

As they descended further, noises of the festive public reached their ears. Loud music and chants bellowed from different sources resulting in dissonant sounds. Vendors of all sorts and beggars of every age and gender contributed to this cacophony. Though the sounds from the entire square outside the gate were already deafening, the shrieks from the throng were getting louder and louder. It seemed that their celebration would be endless.

Emir Moustafa El-Gandour waited a little before he responded, "The strangest thing of all is that we accepted an invitation without any planned activity or conditions. We just said we're coming and unbelievably here we are!"

Another *Emir*, who was listening to their conversation, said laughingly, "Gentlemen, don't be so fastidious. In a few moments, we'll be out of that gate and, believe you me, I'll not participate in any damn parade. Instead, I'll go home and surround myself with my women."

As soon as the ceremonial Albanian cavalry leading the procession passed through the Bab Al-Azab gate and were actually outside, they stopped. On direct orders from their commander, they dismounted and faced the gate. Suddenly, an extraordinarily loud military drumbeat prevailed over all the noises. The rumble could even be heard by the last Mameluke poised at the top of the slope.

"What does that mean? Why have they stopped and blocked the gate? Let us charge out of this place!" shouted a furious *Emir*.

"Is that some kind of goodbye ceremony that they were supposed to perform at the top?" questioned another jokingly.

Abruptly, the military sounds of the drums stopped. To everyone's surprise, an Albanian commander shouted orders in a clear and loud voice.

"Orders! Close the Bab Al-Azab gate. Orders! Close the Bab Al-Azab gate."

Taken by a complete surprise, the chief *Emirs* and the Mamelukes froze on their horses as the huge Bab Al-Azab gate was slammed shut in their faces. They were instantly threatened with the undisputable reality of being trapped in a narrow passage between two extremely massive high walls with no possible means of escape. Absolute silence and stillness prevailed amongst them. They were motionless and speechless yet curious and fearless of what was to come. They drew their swords with one hand and their muskets with the other, waiting courageously to encounter the unexpected.

22

With no trace of compassion or warning, the gates of hell abruptly opened its blazing flames. As originally planned, it happened rapidly, wickedly and unpredictably. Only one man could have plotted and planned such an atrocity so perfectly: the Pasha. Only when all basic elements of humanity are suspended or ignored, could such a horrific act be carried out. Life became null and void, a triumph for evil and immorality. The earth stopped spinning, the sun froze, and the moon was mortified to witness it. Time had no meaning as time and history were ashamed to record such a despicable act. Devils celebrated, angels lamented, and people wondered what other possible horrors could follow.

The moment the Bab Al-Azab gate was slammed shut, orders immediately came down to officer Zamarawy. Though the orders were direct and clear, he was still confused and perplexed. He shouted as loud as he could muster at his deputies to command soldiers to fire on whatever was down below in the passage. With their muskets ready and loaded, the soldiers peered over the wall down at the narrow passage. To their astonishment and disbelief from high above, they saw hundreds of alarmed *Emirs* and Mamelukes helplessly trapped on their agitated horses. Despite their brutal and ferocious nature, the Albanian soldiers hesitated then looked at their deputies and their commander with uncertainty. Surprisingly, the Albanian unit realized that they still had held some consideration for humanity and military principles. Even though they regularly slaughtered and robbed innocent people, their conscience at this moment was slightly shaken. They knew that it was not right and it was not their duty. It was unquestionably cold-blooded assassination. That much they knew.

Frustrated, Zamarawy shouted at his soldiers, "Shoot, you sons of bitches. What has happened to your ears? Shoot! Shoot!"

Again, and again, aggravated Zamarawy yelled at his soldiers, "Fire, you sons of whores! Fire! Fire!"

Finally, a hail of bullets burst down indiscriminately from atop both towering walls. Whistling as they roared through the air and accompanied with blasting echoes from their source, the bullets lethally reached their targets: an *Emir*, a Mameluke, a footman, a servant, or even a horse.

Emirs and Mamelukes ensnared below saw the muskets aimed directly at them and parts of the Albanian soldiers' headgear. Their panicked horses moved in circles and jumped frantically. Some Mamelukes fell to the ground while others were trampled under hoofs. A few Mamelukes bravely shouted at the Albanians, "You treacherous cowards. Come down here and fight like true men!"

Others waved their swords and shot their muskets in the air while bellowing, "We'll find you all in hell and we'll cut your roasted bodies for the rats."

A few Mamelukes attempted the impossible task of climbing up the walls to fight the soldiers only to be shot in the process. Others noticed the door to the *harem* and knocked hard and loud seeking protection. The doors remained closed and the massacre continued. Many Mamelukes, resigned to their fate, began to pray, entreating God for his mercy, imploring his forgiveness, and pleading for Paradise.

As a result, rivers of blood began to flow rapidly in all directions. Fragments of human bones and flesh were carried along the stream. Some bullets found a body and remained embedded into it. Other bullets went through several bodies before ending their murderess trajectory. The scene became more gruesome with each passing moment. Mercy and compassion were suspended. While the soldiers hesitated at the start, for some strange reason they gradually became more frenzied about their devilish task. They reloaded their guns efficiently and aimed wildly at their helpless targets. Periodically, they even laughed and ridiculed how some Mamelukes took their gunshots. While Zamarawy was inspecting his battalion, he encouraged them further by alluding to the rewards awaiting them. A soldier said to one of his teammates, "The more I shoot, the more I see more of them alive. Is it going to end?"

"It may take a few hours but we'll finish them all," replied another.

During the mayhem, *Emir* Moustafa El-Gandour looked up and saw several muskets aimed at him from above. He raised his sword, ready to welcome his mortal end. His thoughts went to his wife and his newly-circumcised young boy. An image of the debate that had been held at his palace regarding this bloody invitation flashed through his mind. The wickedness of Mohammed Ali's smile emerged clearer than ever to him. He thought that he should have killed him an hour earlier. *Emir* Moustafa El-Gandour's left arm had been torn off by a bullet yet he sensed no pain. Again, he thought of his wife and son while a second bullet hit his chest. Still, he felt no pain. He then saw the heads of two Mamelukes shatter. Blood gushed everywhere over bloody patches already on the ground. In disbelief, he saw two Mameluke bodies fall over others who had already earned a

similar fate. While *Emir* Moustafa El-Gandour observed a
wounded Mameluke desperately trying to protect himself under a
dead horse, another bullet struck his right shoulder. Moustafa El-
Gandour could no longer hold his sword, let alone remain on his
horse. He fell to his knees with a bullet in his chest while his
right shoulder shattered. Tears streamed down his cheeks while
his legs sank into the warm blood of hundreds of other fellow
Mamelukes. All his senses began to fade away, and return. He
thought: *It is only a bad dream. No, it is real*! He confirmed the
horror around him. *Emir* Moustafa El-Gandour was already dead
when his head exploded from the force of two more bullets.

Silky, elegant clothes, embroidered with gold, stylishly
decorated saddles, ornamented swords, and most of all, people in
the prime of their lives simply sank and vanished into a quagmire
of bloody entrails. All disintegrated into nothing and in the end
for nothing. A few centuries of Mameluke history, justified or
unjustified, were erased with blood, their own blood. It was a
cowardly, bleak massacre justified by one ruthless, ambitious
man, Mohammed Ali Pasha!

Brutal and inhuman, the shooting fiercely continued for
hours even after all Mamelukes and their horses were butchered
and dismembered many times over. Death itself was exhausted
from so much killing through a massacre which was so successful
strategically. The only thing left to do was to collect all valuables
from the corpses. Although the Albanian soldiers knew that the
Pasha's rewards were forthcoming, they rushed impatiently like
vultures to search the carcasses of the dead.

As the sounds of the fusillades and agonies of painful
death continued into the night, the celebrations outside the walls
came to a bleak halt. People held their breaths as they were
overwhelmed by the incredible number of shots that could only
be interpreted by one word, Death!

Up at the reception hall eagerly awaiting the outcome, Mohammed Ali's grim face had slightly changed when his Italian doctor announced that it was time to celebrate. It has been alleged that, only then, Mohammed Ali Pasha had simply asked for a glass of water.

23

By nature and tradition, the people of Egypt in general and of Cairo in particular, have always recognized their love and appreciation for all forms of art. As far back as the times of the Pharaohs, music, singing, and dancing have always captivated their hearts and souls. Whenever an occasion presented itself, their artistic persona came to life. The celebrations undertaken by Mohammed Ali Pasha for his son's departure were a reason to indulge and rejoice. The people of Cairo trusted the cause and wished the Pasha and his son, Tousoun, victory and success in whatever their mission may be in Arabia. Believing in generosity, goodwill, and happiness, they wholeheartedly and genuinely took part joyfully in the festivities. No one had ever imagined that a conspiracy was behind it all.

At every square, circle upon circle of people surrounded musicians, dancers, snake charmers, and magicians. The masses danced to the rhythmic beat performed by local artists. Joy and happiness bonded them. Delicious food was served to all, rich and poor alike. Magicians, fire eaters, and monkey trainers offered their best performances to entertain a happy public.

Colourfully dressed, professional dancers performed at the center of a crowded square and there was, as usual, the occasional attempt by a spectator to join in for a few moments as an expression of admiration and approval. In other squares, groups of *darweeshes,* members of a religious order, dressed in their special costumes and pointy head covers, began to twirl while other groups performed *zikr*, twisting their bodies from right to left and left to right while saying *Allah* aloud. Smiling faces, sparkling eyes, and clapping hands demonstrated the delight that the Cairenes were experiencing. Fragrant incense filled the air dispersing sweet-smelling jasmine. At this moment of ecstasy and pleasure, no one thought of how it all had started and no one questioned when it would end. Bliss and contentment were to last forever, or so everyone thought.

When they saw the formation of ceremonial Albanian cavalry, the festive throng near the Bab Al-Azab gate spontaneously applauded. They thought that the anticipated procession was about to begin. The perimeter of the square and both sides of the road in front of the gate were jammed with people with high expectations. Since the French departure, they had not seen a military procession going to war. They were also anxious to see Mohammed Ali Pasha alongside his brave son, Tousoun, who would lead this fighting army to Arabia. Cheering women and girls crowded the rooftops. Many were also peering through the *mashrabiya,* a window enclosed with carved wood latticework that allowed them to see but not to be seen.

While biting on a loaf of bread filled with meat, a bystander asked, "Why don't the Albanians move forward?"

"They're probably waiting for a signal from their commander," answered another.

"That's strange! Why are they closing the gate if the procession is supposed to begin?" a third onlooker questioned.

"They closed the gate!" a few others shouted.

Although celebrations could still be heard from afar, those near the Bab Al-Azab gate began to be concerned. They were accustomed to the angry and spiteful looks of the Albanian cavalry faces. This time there was something plastered on the soldiers' expressions that the crowd could not decipher. The echoes of music and laughter could still be heard from a distance, but those near the Bab Al-Azab gate suddenly became motionless and silent. In their hearts, they felt the torment of the unknown that was about to strike at their very souls. Helpless, unarmed, yet brave and resilient, they stood waiting for the mystery to reveal itself. Suddenly and unexpectedly, the unknown answer to all their questions came from within the Citadel. The answer was two-fold: first, the blast of thousands of bullets being fired and, second, the agony and anguish of the victims being hit. As the shooting intensified, festivities all over the city gradually halted. An absolute silence overcame the masses as their fears increased. Suddenly, an Albanian cavalry appeared from nowhere waving their swords in the air and threatening death. They moved at an incredible speed towards the crowds. Clearing the streets became the only option of survival for the people. There was no doubt among Cairenes that the Mamelukes trapped inside the Citadel were the targets.

Clearing the main thoroughfares, the masses vanished as quickly as they had assembled. They later realized that they were not what the brutal soldiers were after. Homes and palaces of the Mamelukes were the prime targets of the hoarding soldiers. The Albanian military violently and outrageously broke into the Mamelukes' households with orders to slaughter each and every Mameluke left in Cairo. As an additional task, the soldiers took it upon themselves to rob all valuables including taking possession of wives and concubines. They also gave themselves the right to raid any other households of well-to-do Egyptians. The tragedy in the making began by the occupying Ottoman army permitting itself to rob and massacre helpless citizens.

Hundreds of *Emirs* and Mamelukes were cold bloodedly massacred at the Citadel. Hundreds of others were slaughtered wherever else they were found in the city. Mohammed Ali Pasha's soldiers had orders to continue killing any Mameluke found alive. The soldiers acted as the ultimate, unstoppable authority capable of doing just about anything. As they entered palaces or homes of Mamelukes or even ordinary Egyptians, they slaughtered guards and servants. The soldiers raped women or captured them as slaves and pillaged all valuables. There were no boundaries to what the soldiers would or would not do. They acted as if they had an absolute right to possess and take ownership of the city and its inhabitants.

The festive atmosphere that reigned over the city a few hours earlier had been unpredictably transformed into an appalling violation of humanity. People ran to their homes seeking refuge in complete horror and dismay. The poor and destitute sought shelter in the narrow congested lanes or piles of rubbish that they could find. Gates to narrow streets were closed. Rooftops were deserted and all windows were immediately shut. Suppressed wailing and crying could be heard from every home and everyone thought that doomsday had arrived in full force. To all, the spectre of death loomed over them diminishing all vitality and beauty. The acrid stench of blood, the sound of suffering, the agony of realizing one's vulnerability, and the brutality of absolute power and supremacy were the only truths of the day.

The soldiers proudly paraded the skinned heads of slaughtered Mamelukes which they had mounted on spears. They raced triumphantly towards the Citadel to collect their rewards from the Pasha. People, frightened and apprehensive, witnessed the unfolding disaster from their hiding places. Inside and outside the Citadel, the victors systematically continued to collect and skin the heads of the fallen Mamelukes.

The day following the massacre and near the entrance to the Citadel, passers-by could see, to their horror, the hundreds of spears supporting skinned heads on exhibit as proof of victory. The Mameluke rule of Egypt, which had lasted for a few centuries, had just ended in the most evil tragedy imaginable.

24

One shot whizzed near his left ear and a couple of others had almost reached his horse as Zafaran *Bey* suddenly found himself suspended in mid-air shouting aloud, "There is no God but Allah and Mohammed is his Prophet!" While he felt that his heart seemed to be moving upward, he instinctively tightened his grip on the harness with all his might. Harder and harder Zafaran *Bey* clutched his horse while his sense of reality began to fade away. His mind raced much faster than his descending speed. A strange reverberation of air filled his eardrums propelling him into a new and extraordinary world of silence. His vision blurred with unwanted tears yet he could still see the many minarets of Cairo below. His horse galloped in a desperate attempt to touch familiar ground but to no avail. Images of Zafaran *Bey*'s wife and children flashed constantly before his eyes urgently imploring him to come and join them. Suddenly, a feeling of cold and nakedness overwhelmed him as his headgear and scarf flew upward. Despite his distorted vision, he could see and sense how fast he was descending in relation to the stone blocks of the Citadel wall from which he had just leapt. He wished that he had wings to help him reverse his predestined direction. Descending at high speed gave him a sense of being bodiless as well as mindless. Overwhelmed and perplexed, he saw himself with his head blown up juxtaposed with another vision of his head smashed on the ground next to his horse. Many more apparitions kept racing through his mind. For some reason, he believed that nothing had been real. In some sense, he felt that he no longer existed. He concluded that what was happening was simply an experience in his afterlife.

The agonizing and excruciating shock to the horse when they both finally hit the ground was beyond description. In less than a second, each and every bone of the enormous and magnificent beast had been crushed and crushed again. The stench of blood muddied with dust caused Zafaran *Bey* to cough hard almost to the point of suffocation. Conscious of himself being still alive, he started to control his breathing and looked around to reassure his senses that he was still on earth. At a fair distance, he saw an old Bedouin approaching him cautiously. Remaining on the ground, Zafaran *Bey* gradually eased himself off his dead steed and waited for the old man.

For many years, Hag Abu Ragab, like a handful of other Bedouin and beggars, took refuge near the highest wall of the Citadel. They had found peace and security in the middle of nowhere and far from the gates, roads, or streets. Their tents or huts were scruffy so no one paid any attention as no one else had been there in the first place. They knew one another yet they never even bothered to acknowledge or greet one another except in rare instances. Occasionally, one would leave for weeks or even months and yet all his little belongings remained untouched until he returned.

Though it was unusual to hear a continuous fusillade that seemed endless, Hag Abu Ragab had not been distracted or disturbed by it. He knew that whatever took place in the Citadel had never concerned him. Suddenly, a heavy and unusual thud reached his ears. He stepped out of his tent and immediately saw a man atop a trampled horse.

"I heard so many guns! Were they all shooting at you? And now that you're down here, why are they still shooting up there?" asked Hag Abu Ragab.

Zafaran *Bey* looked at the man for a while, and then said, "They are killing all of us. All of us!"

The old Bedouin rushed to help Zafaran *Bey* to his feet and assisted him towards his tent. He sat him carefully on a mat then asked in surprise, "They're still shooting forcefully? How many of you are they killing?" He stopped speaking for a while as he warily examined Zafaran *Bey*. The Bedouin continued, "Your horse saved you, though you've got some minor injuries. The poor creature is shattered but you're alive! Thank God for that! The horse's huge body served well to protect you. Look! You're safe and alive. Though I'm sure they believe you're dead, just in case, I'll place a cover over the dead beast. Then we'll see what to do next."

He placed a roll of material under his arm, retrieved a few long poles, and left his tent. He first looked up at the colossal wall and was convinced that no one up there would even bother to look down below. The neighbourhood was deserted as the deafening echo, along with the unpleasant odour of gunpowder, made it hard to breathe. Skilfully and efficiently, the old Bedouin placed a temporary cover over the dead beast. To his surprise, he heard other gunshots emanating from the city centre as well. He then concluded that the targets were not only Mamelukes inside the Citadel but also all others in the city.

Consciously and for the first time, Zafaran *Bey* could clearly hear the sound of bullets and the anguish of those receiving them. It was agonizing for him to realize that he was alive and could not help his comrades. Tears filled his eyes when he thought of his wife and children. In retrospect, he had suspected that a malicious trap had been veiled by that invitation from Mohammed Ali yet never could he, in his wildest dreams, have imagined such perfidy. Even the devil, himself, he thought, would never have been able to come up with such terror. With both hands on his ears, he tried to block the never-ending cacophony of bullets and the tortuous cries of his fellow Mamelukes.

The old Bedouin returned to the tent with the saddle on his shoulder and Zafaran *Bey*'s sword under his left arm. With an inquisitive look he stated, "They're still shooting and viciously slaughtering your people. What did you folks do to deserve such horrific punishment? From afar, I can see ordinary people running for shelter and help in all directions. If I remember correctly, it was supposed to be a day of celebration. Before, I could hear singing and music. Now this! This massacre is a sign of greed for control and power."

Zafaran *Bey* looked at the ground, shook his head, and exclaimed, "It's a misguided decision. We shouldn't have come to the Citadel in the first place. It's far too late to even think about it now. Who's to blame now and what's the point anyway?"

The old Bedouin fetched and found a clay beaker and handed Zafaran *Bey* some water, then calmly and thoughtfully asked, "Do you have a family?"

"Yes. Now I miss them more than ever. I should have never left them. It's entirely my fault. I should have died with the others. Why am I still here?"

The old Bedouin calmly replied, "This is the will of God Almighty. God saved you for your family, young man. Don't be ungrateful and thank God. Get up! Wash and give praise to God and demonstrate your thanks! Pray!"

Zafaran *Bey* wiped his eyes while still staring at the ground and uttered, "Hopefully, by now, my family has arrived at the encampment of my dear friend, Salama."

"Salama?" inquired the old man.

"Yes, do you know him?"

"Of course, I know him and I know his father as well. My tribe intermarried with his. We're like one family. Do you want to get there?"

"Of course, and now, if possible!" declared Zafaran *Bey*.

"Look here. What's your name, son?"

"Zafaran. Zafaran *Bey*! I was with *Emir* Moustafa El-Gandour when it all started up there. I believe I'm the only one who managed to jump off the towering wall."

"Zafaran *Bey*? I've heard of you and I know *Emir* Moustafa El-Gandour well. May God bless his soul, if we may say so now?"

"May God bless their souls and open his wide Paradise for them all!"

"Let me tell you this," said the old man in a low voice, "I know how anxious you are to join your family and so, let us deal with the situation cool-headedly. Luckily, none of my Bedouin or beggar neighbours noticed your fall; otherwise, they would all be here. The only one who knows about you is me and we want to keep it that way. Don't you agree?"

"Yes, of course," replied Zafaran *Bey*.

With seemingly no end in sight, the distressing sounds of fusillades and the agonies of painful death of men and beasts continued. The conversation stopped for a few minutes. The old man then whispered, "Well then! Here's the plan. You stay here until we know which way the world is going." With a faint smile, the old Bedouin continued, "You'll wash all blood stains off your body, burn all your clothes, and wear some of mine. When possible, I'll try to buy you a mule and some food for your trip."

At this, Zafaran *Bey* pulled a small purse off his waist and handed it to the old man who simply took it and stuck it carelessly into his pocket.

"Possibly in a couple of days, I'll accompany you through the poor part of the city until we reach the western gate. Once you pass through it, I suppose you would then know your way. Are you armed?"

"Yes, I carry a loaded pistol, a dagger, and a sword."

"Your weapons are too elegant and expensive for a peasant leaving the city. I suggest that you roll them into this piece of material and that you only take them out if you need to defend yourself. For now, sleep on that mat over there. You may need a good rest to prepare for the days ahead of you."

"Will you pass though the city gate with me or will you just watch me from afar?"

"If you want, I could accompany you even to Salama's encampment. But I promised some merchants to meet with them in the city in a few days. We Bedouin have our ways in dealing with all kinds of people including those at the city gates. It is enough for them to see me wishing you *Salam* (peace) on your trip. May God be with you, son!"

"I have great trust in God and in you!"

"Have a good night despite what has happened and is still occurring throughout the city."

It took Zafaran *Bey* a few hours to come to terms with the fate of his comrades and the fact that he was alive. Sleep finally overpowered his despair and hopelessness. When he awoke the following day, gunshots from the Citadel had ceased yet hundreds could still be clearly heard coming from different parts of the city.

25

Carefully using the dim light of a tiny oil lamp, Awaad and Mahroos explored and selected the best of the very best in the hidden room they occupied. Narrow shelves and small drawers were loaded with diamonds, jewellery, and gold coins. It was hard to believe and even harder to imagine that they were surrounded by such riches. Mahroos thought that even if they filled all their baggy clothes, there would still be more left for several other furtive trips. He also thought that he would never be able in his lifetime to spend even a little portion of what he was carrying. The fact that puzzled his mind was that so much wealth had been accumulated, left hidden, and untouched. When the sound of jubilant celebration stopped, people's frightful howls became clear and the smoke from gunfire began to reach his nostrils. All such pleasant thoughts of the treasure vanished from his mind.

"Something is definitely not right out there and I don't like it," shouted Awaad.

"Possibly, Mamelukes and some soldiers got into a fight or perhaps the French are back. Let's get on with what we're here for, don't you think?" proposed Mahroos while trying to push more loot into his already filled pockets.

"Can't you hear it? It's obviously an endless fusillade from afar. Clear shots can also be heard from nearby palaces. Possibly, our turn could be soon! Still don't ...."

Before Awaad could finish his sentence, shots being fired inside the palace they were in could clearly be heard. Women and children screamed frightfully as they ran through the corridors. The two interlopers also distinctly heard the loud footsteps and harsh shouts of Albanian soldiers as they followed on the heels of the terrified women and children.

Awaad motioned to Mahroos to remain inside the storage room at the same time he held the sword handle ready to close off the space, if needed. Suddenly, they looked at each other as the door swung open and a screaming young woman threw herself inside. Impulsively, Awaad pulled the handle to immediately lock the wall enclosing the treasure.

"Remove those bangles or I'll chop your arms off," a soldier shouted at a frantic and frightened young woman.

Awaad and Mahroos heard a loud scream followed by struggle and movements. Another soldier shouted seemingly from outside the room, "There are no Mamelukes to be found here in this palace. The owner and his followers must have already been killed at the Citadel. Hurry! We have to move on to other palaces. Hurry! Time is limited and there is still a lot to do."

When Awaad was sure that only one soldier remained in the room with the woman, he pulled the handle and the wall opened. He walked slowly to the far end of the room and saw a soldier about to hack off the arm of a young woman. Awaad's mind raced and searched for a way to save the helpless soul and, at the same time, he was evaluating what the other soldier had just said. Undoubtedly, he concluded that a major disaster was in progress outside the palace.

While ready at any moment to pull out his musket, Awaad courageously and casually said, "I'm looking for *Emir* Moustafa El-Gandour. Do you know where to find him?"

"And who the hell are you? Don't you see that I'm busy here?" bellowed the soldier while holding his sword in the air and aiming at the woman's arm.

"I'm a merchant. I have a special and personal delivery for the *Emir*. Can you please tell me where he is?" Awaad answered indifferently while pretending to ignore the soldier's vicious tone and cruel demeanour.

"Get out of my sight or I'll stab you before I finish my job with this bitch. What kind of special delivery have you got anyway?"

Again a loud voice came from the corridor, "We're leaving now. Join us at the next palace. Hurry!"

Releasing the young woman, the soldier stood up with his sword pointed at Awaad, then shouted towards the corridor, "All right. I'll join you shortly." He then turned his bearded face towards Awaad and said, "Did you hear me? I've just asked you a question. What kind of special delivery do you have?"

Still calm and seemingly disinterested Awaad responded, "I've already told you that it's a private matter for the *Emir*!"

"It seems like you're as stupid as a donkey! The *Emir* and all the others have been slaughtered at the Citadel. Now they're all in hell and I intend to send you along to join them soon after you tell me where and what is that special delivery you've got." The Albanian moved a few steps forward with his sword pointed at Awaad's heart.

Awaad quickly began to assess the situation. Most Mamelukes had been massacred at the Citadel and Mohammed Ali's soldiers were hunting for the rest of them. The city was in certain turmoil and disarray. Impulsively and decisively, Awaad pulled out his musket and shot the soldier in the face. The sound reverberated throughout the room. The young woman shrieked as fragments of the soldier's skull splattered near her naked legs. Blood gushed from the neck wound of the heavy body as it fell onto the floor. At the same instant, Awaad rushed to the terrified woman and held her mouth to stop her endless wailing. She only stopped when he calmly said, "Hold your shrieks or we'll all be dead!"

Mahroos finally appeared from behind the open wall. In disbelief, he looked at the bleeding, headless soldier and the terrified woman. He thought of his wife and children and cursed his decision to accept this horrific escapade. He was about to utter something when Awaad motioned to him to stop. He pointed at the wall sword handle and signalled to Mahroos to pull it to close the wall before the woman could realize what she was seeing. Mahroos pulled the handle reluctantly and the wall moved back into place.

Awaad quietly questioned the woman, "Where is everybody?"

Frightened and still shaken, she replied, "They all fled the palace when they saw the soldiers coming in. I don't know where they all went. By the time I was about to leave, that one saw my bangles and he came after me." She pointed at the man in the pool of blood.

"Look! We all want to get out of here safely. Do you know where the stable is? We need horses or donkeys to get away fast."

"Yes! I think it's at the other end of the yard."

The three walked out of the room into the corridor. They could clearly hear hundreds of shots being fired, sounds of anguish, and people screaming for shelter. The palace seemed lifeless and deserted. The young woman noticed the apparent difficulty in the way Awaad and Mahroos walked. She might have attributed it to many reasons but it never crossed her mind that they were carrying loot more than double their own weight. When they finally reached the stable, Awaad had some difficulty unchaining the door. Inside, they found well-groomed horses and some mules.

"Horses may draw attention. We'll take mules. You'll ride with me. If possible, I'll drop you at a friend's *kahn* where you'll be safe," said Awaad to the still horrified woman.

He then helped her scramble up and sit behind him on the already overburdened mule.

"Hold on tightly! It isn't going to be simple," cautioned Awaad.

It was almost dark by the time they left the palace grounds. The repeated reverberation of gunfire accompanied them throughout their journey. The young woman tried hard to suppress her crying. Though it would take longer, Mahroos suggested riding through the back alleys of the poorest districts to avoid encountering soldiers. The ride seemed endless and their loads felt heavier by the minute. From time to time, they could hear soldiers attacking palaces and killing Mamelukes in the distance.

Stars and nearly a half moon twinkled brightly in the clear skies above them. The mules could hardly move any faster and it was well after midnight when they finally reached Awaad's home. A terrified servant opened the huge door and was relieved when he saw his master dismounting the mule.

Awaad asked a female servant to take care of the young woman until morning while he and Mahroos entered a room near the reception hall. Once inside, they were relieved and emptied their laden pockets carefully into a wooden chest. Awaad secured the chest with an extraordinary lock and gave the key to Mahroos. Then he said rather flippantly, "To go back now and bring the rest would definitely be the right thing to do!"

Awaad threw himself on a nearby pillow and fell asleep. Mahroos placed the key into a pocket inside his underwear and arranged a few soft pillows for himself near a wall. Completely exhausted, he stretched his drained body to welcome sleep but to no avail. He thought of the night before when he was among the joyful, celebrating Mamelukes. He also remembered that only one week earlier, he had been with his wife and children. He profoundly understood that he must prepare himself for the horror he might face the next day.

The following day and according to their agreement, Awaad and Mahroos divided the biggest score they had ever made. With complete caution and care, Mahroos loaded his share into a creatively designed double sack made especially for him by his friend, Awaad. The inside sack contained his share of the valuables. The outer bag was filled with old clothes and other items that no one would ever care to look at.

"One of my servants just informed me that the killing of Mamelukes is still happening in different parts of the city. Also, the dates for caravans leaving Cairo are unknown. You're very welcome to stay here till we get some good news," Awaad suggested.

"Many thanks for everything but I really prefer to return to Zeyad Abu Ali's *kahn* and wait there. Thank God we've got the mules from last night. Do you mind if I take one of them?"

Awaad smiled then replied, "Of course, I don't mind! They are yours just as mine. Take both of them, if you need to. By the way, the girl from yesterday seems quite happy here. She's been taken care of by the female servants. She'll stay for now and then in a few days, I'll let her decide for herself what she wants to do."

"Luckily, the *kahn* isn't far from here. I assure you that I'll send you word once safely back home with my family."

"And, I assure you that if there is any future adventure in sight, you'll be the first to know about it."

They shook hands and parted.

Though endless gun shots and cries could be heard throughout the city, Mahroos reached the *kahn* unharmed. In a hurry, a terrified servant took his mule to the backyard and vanished. Seaham magically opened the main door and Mahroos walked in carrying his heavy sack on his shoulder. Despite the bright sun outside, it seemed dim in the main corridor where frightened Seaham stood motionless as a statue. Impulsively, she threw herself at Mahroos and began to lavish him wildly with kisses while feverishly babbling, "I'm glad you're alive. I'm happy you're back. They're killing everyone and they'll kill us too."

"Seaham, don't be afraid. I'm here with you now. Don't be afraid, love, they're only after Mamelukes."

"Master Zeyad Abu Ali hasn't been here for two days and we don't know what to do anymore."

Calmly and kindly, Mahroos reassured her, "Just relax and be yourself. Let's go to my room and talk. First, could you please get me something to eat? I'm really hungry."

Once inside his room, Mahroos quickly and carefully extracted a handful of golden coins from the hidden inner sack. From under his belt, he pulled out a small empty purse and placed the glittering coins into it. An hour later, Seaham entered with a tray loaded with food.

"How did you manage yesterday and last night? I was so worried."

"I had no other choice. I stayed with Awaad."

"The servant told me that you came on a mule. I guess you couldn't find any donkey boys, considering the situation."

"Yes. Awaad gave it to me as a gift just in case I missed the caravan and still would have to make my way home."

Seaham worriedly suggested, "I think it's better for you to wait until a caravan is available to take you back home. Don't you think? I would not take any chances with those malicious Ottoman soldiers."

"You just want me to stay here with you. Say it!"

"Of course, I want you to stay, but I also know that you already have a family waiting for you. All I really want is your safety, and when you have an opportunity in the future, come back and stay with us."

For two days Mahroos remained at the *kahn* while Seaham entertained and amused him with her charm and beauty. On the third day, Zeyad Abu Ali entered with the much awaited news, "Authority and discipline are restored and many caravans are ready to depart."

Two donkey boys awaited Mahroos to take him to the caravan. Before leaving his room, Mahroos hugged and kissed Seaham. He then carefully placed the small purse, which he had earlier filled with golden coins, in her bosom.

26

The two young Abyssinian concubines at Zamarawy's household were not only beautiful but also clever. Although they gave the impression of being twins, Haliema and Gamiela were from two different tribes. Though they spoke the same language, each had a slightly different accent. Despite Zamarawy's rough and careless treatment, especially in the morning, they had been quite contented living with him. They had become accustomed to his daily routine and accepted it. In fact, they were treated like ladies while many other servants, household personnel, and slaves did all the housework. Their main task was to look after officer Zamarawy: wake him up in the morning to wash and dress him before he left, in the evening to serve him wine, stuff his water-pipe with tobacco mixed with hashish and, of course, satisfy his many other desires. Rarely did they enjoy fulfilling his wild and irrational needs. They knew his occasional wild fondness only too well of positioning their tiny bodies close enough to enjoy penetration with each of them.

Haliema and Gamiela loved the city, its markets, and the people on the streets. At their age, their restricted life was unbearable. Their strong desire to find men to marry and have a family was overwhelming. They were ready to give up their own lives for freedom and to lead a normal life. They prepared themselves for that cherished day to unfold when they could leave Zamarawy's house forever. Freedom became their dream and passion.

Their early days with Zamarawy had been terrifying. The only person that sympathized and understood their agony was Nafiesa, an elderly woman who worked as a cook and also served their daily meals. Nafiesa came to the house early every morning and left before sunset. She was an excellent cook and a caring woman. She understood the predicament in which the two young girls found themselves and tried to support them whenever she could. Over time, she gained their confidence and trust. Once she told them that drinking wine was religiously *haram* (forbidden). The girls never touched any spirits ever again. Another time she told them that being an unmarried concubine was unacceptable, which made them occasionally resent Zamarawy. They even asked him to legally marry them both. Of course, he laughed and ironically, as punishment, he refused to see them for two days. On rare occasions, they were allowed to go out with Nafiesa and buy clothes. In confidence, they told her about their idea of escaping to freedom. At first, Nafiesa was hesitant. She then later told them that whatever they decided, they could always come to her house as a start on the road to freedom. Thereafter, whenever they had the opportunity to go out, she made a special detour to her house so that they would know how to get there whenever possible in the future.

Unusually late that night and after he had participated in commanding the massacre of the Mamelukes at the Citadel, Zamarawy dismounted his horse, dismissed his six guards, and went into the reception room. His two beautiful Abyssinian concubines were still waiting for him: one with a large glass of wine and, the other, with a glowing water-pipe loaded with his favourite hashish and ready for imbibing. His weary, angry look was not unusual but something else seemed to have altered his personality altogether. He threw himself on a pillow and sat while one of the girls politely placed a cushion against the wall behind his back. He then lifted the large wine glass and drank its contents. He stretched out his heavy arm with the empty glass and Gamiela poured more of the ruby-red liquid into it from a huge bottle neatly embedded into a beautifully woven basket. As he vigorously inhaled his favourite smoke, Gamiela continued to refill the large goblet. His thoughts of the massacre disturbed him tremendously. He hated his job. He hated himself and hated life as well. He hit his head several times against the wall then suddenly calmed down. Subsequently, and as the girls had anticipated, a faint smile shaped his lips. While the girls enjoyed breathing the invigorating smoke, normally at that stage, they would drop their silky gowns, undress him, and willingly submit to his desires. From past experience, however, they realized that the faint smile they had observed hid some mysterious meaning that they both could not decipher. Carefully, the young women communicated only with their eyes and finally concluded that they should replenish the wine and re-stuff the water-pipe. They were surprised by Zamarawy's depressed look and his unprecedented endless desire to drink and smoke. After a while, the glass fell out of Zamarawy's hand onto the carpet. His eyes closed and his usual loud snoring began to echo throughout the hall. They both realized that finally an opportunity had presented itself for them to leave. The guards had been dismissed and likely had joined other soldiers in the looting frenzy. All servants had left and were possibly hiding in their homes. The slaves had been confined to their quarters and would certainly never interfere with them. They decided to execute what they believed to be their perfect escape plan which had been ready for months. Wearing street clothes, while each carried a small sack of belongings, they rushed to the back door. In the courtyard, they climbed halfway up the slightly bent palm tree. They then jumped over the fence into the narrow lane behind the house. From that point, they knew exactly how to reach Nafiesa's home and walked clinging to one another. From afar in the darkness, they could hear many galloping hoofs, shouting soldiers, endless shooting, and tormented people. The sound of loud gunshots frightened them so much that they almost abandoned their plan. Finally, when they reached Nafiesa's lane, its gate was closed. In desperation, the two girls kept knocking on the wooden structure to no avail. They suddenly heard a voice which came from the other side, "Who are you and what do you want?"

In a weary and frightened whisper, Haliema replied in her accent, "We want to see Nafiesa. She lives in this lane. She's expecting us. Please let us in!"

"No one with such a name lives here. Just go away!"

Begging in desperation, Gamiela replied, "We're lost and afraid. Have mercy on us! Let us in. Please! Soldiers may shoot and kill us!"

No response returned and it seemed that the gate keeper had left his post. They began to cry and sob like two lost kittens. Suddenly, they heard the reassuring voice of a woman from an open window.

"What's troubling you girls? Do you need any help?" the woman inquired.

The two girls looked at each other and answered in a unanimous voice, "We're looking for Nafiesa who lives in this lane!"

"Well, she lives two houses down from here. She's probably asleep. Let me wake her up and she'll open the gate for you."

A few minutes later, Nafiesa opened the door and took the two girls into her arms. The three cried of joy and happiness as they entered her house.

27

For all pushcart transporters and cleaners, the morning following the gruesome slaughter of hundreds of Mamelukes started as a grisly and horrific day. While breathing gradually became difficult in the entire district near the Citadel, it took only minutes after sunrise for the stench of death to extend even beyond its perimeter. The logistics of disposing of countless corpses as well as fragmented parts of men and beasts appeared to be an impossible undertaking. While workers were anxious to start and complete the dreadful mission, soldiers were insistent to scrutinize and methodically search each and every corpse for plunder. In addition, soldiers sought to find heads of well-known Mameluke leaders in order to get the special rewards promised by the Pasha. The situation was viewed differently by transporters and cleaners who were in a hurry to accomplish what seemed to be an endless grisly chore. Each group interfered with the other to the point that another massacre seemed likely. In the end and still miserable from the night before, Zamarawy and the other three officers ordered their deputies to give the soldiers two hours to search for booty and Mameluke heads. Thereafter, they must report to the garrison.

Once the two hours had elapsed, the soldiers reluctantly left the scene as each carried enough valuables sufficient for many years to come. Some soldiers skinned human heads and mounted them on spears. They then displayed the macabre trophies in front of the Citadel after getting an official receipt from an officer. Deputies and officers kept watchful eyes on soldiers returning to their barracks. Methodically, several units of soldiers walked into their quarters carrying their own spoils. Once inside the barracks, each soldier began to unload the loot into a bag or a wooden box. Though each had been preoccupied with what had been retrieved, their greedy eyes moved swiftly over the loot and examined what others might have accumulated. Gradually, the main issue among soldiers was to compare the quantity and quality of what they had amassed with the booty of their other comrades. Though seemingly each had a considerable amount of riches, shouts of discontent and disappointment could be heard throughout the barracks. An unexpected surly mood of frustration and impatience began to worsen within the soldiers. Suddenly an endless loud roar echoed throughout their quarters with shouts of support and denial.

"I found that studded sword first. You took it away while I had been busy collecting other items. You son of a pig thief," shouted one soldier to another.

"I had it all along. It was the first thing I picked up when I entered the bloody passage," came the reply.

Another soldier exclaimed, "I saw him. He is a cheat! He is a liar."

Shouting began to amplify and the deputies tried to control the situation to no avail. A fist fight began to take place and some soldiers went for their swords. The noise could easily be heard outside the barracks. Officer Zamarawy, still furiously enraged over the sudden disappearance of his two Abyssinian concubines, and horribly affected by his excessive indulgence in wine and hashish the night before, stormed in with two deputies. Disgustedly, he watched the disorder in the making. Surprisingly, no one noticed him as the scuffle continued. Still ignored, Zamarawy took a loaded gun from one of his deputies and fired at the ceiling causing small rocks and dust to fall over the disputing soldiers. Finally, the men realized the presence of their officer and all arguments came to a sudden halt. Zamarawy returned the gun to his deputy and shot an angry look to another who immediately understood and loudly ordered the soldiers to stand at attention and in formation. The soldiers obeyed the command while Zamarawy walked between them stepping purposefully with his boots on their precious spoils. He then returned to the front and faced them.

"You sons of bitches and scum of whores! When will you ever learn? Are you arguing and fighting over what you've picked up from dead animals? Who has a problem? Who didn't get his fair share or has been cheated? Who?"

A young soldier uttered a word in response before a comrade could secretly attempt to hit his elbow as a warning not to speak.

"Have I heard someone say something out there? Has any *one* of you got a grievance or a complaint? Do come forward and I'll solve your problem fairly," Zamarawy demanded.

Brave, unsuspecting, and naïve, the young soldier advanced to the front and stood with full respect in front of his officer.

"My sword was taken from me. I picked it up first. It belongs to me," the young soldier declared.

"And where is that wonderful sword? Bring it here so that we may all admire it."

While all other soldiers held their breath, the young soldier went back, retrieved the sword, and handed it his officer. Zamarawy held the weapon and gave it a trivial look of admiration. He then furiously gave it to one of his deputies and, to everyone's surprise, ordered him to throw the sword out of the window. Turning his blazing eyes to the young baffled soldier, Zamarawy exclaimed, "I'm sure you want a better one than that awful sword and here it is!"

Unpredictably, and with all the strength and energy he could muster, Zamarawy dealt a brutal blow with his huge fist to the young soldier's jaw causing him to roll a few steps away on the hard floor.

Pushcart owners and cleaners began their repulsive mission resentfully, hoping that the soldiers may have overlooked something or other that could be of value to them. At a fair distance from the Citadel, numerous teams of gravediggers and others were working collectively on a massive crater near the Mokattam Hills. In a few of hours, the crater became wider and deeper to hold almost twice as many corpses as were now savagely packed into the wretched and narrow passage at the Citadel. Other teams of workers were clearing a path from the Citadel to the huge fissure for the challenging task of transporting all the bodies.

Transporting carcasses, dumping corpses into the newly-dug gigantic hole, and thoroughly cleaning the narrow passage at the Citadel were assumed by thousands of working men and soldiers. They worked relentlessly all day and a good part of the night. Orders were clear and specific: the passage would be bloodless by the following dawn and all bodies in the crater would be completely covered by sand and earth. Ironically, though hundreds of Mameluke skinned heads were on display outside the Citadel, the intention was to suggest that a massacre had never taken place. Despite the danger of being caught and slaughtered, hundreds of Cairenes, who were hidden from the fray, watched with anguish and dismay at the progress being made.

Zafaran *Bey*, disguised in Bedouin clothes, was no exception. From a distance on the other side of the Citadel, he and the old Bedouin were able to witness the entire procedure through holes in the tent. Helplessly and with eyes filled with sorrow and tears, Zafaran *Bey*'s heart grieved for his fellow

Mamelukes. Though he felt that he had done the right thing by leaping and escaping such a fate as theirs, a sense of disloyalty weighed heavily on his heart.

Even on the third morning after the dreadful massacre, soldiers throughout the city, continued to loot and slaughter anyone who stood in their way. It had been an endless madness and rage not only against the Mamelukes but also against the population. As a result, homes were secured and merchants barricaded their shops. Cairo seemed to be in a state of civil war.

As the vicious conduct by soldiers reached an intolerable stage, a group of religious leaders, acting on behalf of the population, sought protection directly from the Pasha himself. Early that afternoon, drumbeats from the Citadel surprisingly shook the air as thunder roiling through the skies. The Bab Al-Azab gate opened wide and an orderly regiment of soldiers marched peacefully in elegant columns leading the way in a formal procession. The discipline and authority of the regiment imposed a sense of calm and peacefulness. This event enticed the populace to seek the help and security they needed. A regiment of cavalry carrying Turkish flags was followed by what undoubtedly stunned and surprised all the spectators: Mohammed Ali Pasha himself and his son. The Pasha rode proudly on his elegantly decorated horse next to his son, Tousoun. In spite of everyone's knowledge of the grisly massacre, in desperation the people could not help but greet the Pasha warmly. When some merchants courageously presented him with grievances against some soldiers who had looted their establishments, swift orders were given to arrest and slaughter the soldiers immediately. The procession toured and inspected the entire city, thereby re-establishing peace and assuring the citizens of peace, tranquility, and order.

Ironically, while the Pasha was outwardly supporting the citizens of Cairo, troops were being dispatched secretly all over the country to massacre Mamelukes wherever they were, particularly in Upper Egypt. Consequently, most remaining Mamelukes were brutally killed and only a few managed to escape and cross the border into the Sudan.

As a result, life in the city seemed to return to normal; however, neither the city of Cairo nor Egypt as a country would ever be the same again without the Mamelukes.

Though it was much quieter than his first day at the old Bedouin tent, Zafaran *Bey* was surprised to perceive some order in the air. When he awoke from a dreadful and restless second night, it was almost mid-day. The sheepskin bedding he slept in was infested with bugs and the uneven terrain under him caused every bone in his body to ache. Though some of his minor injuries were troublesome, he was certainly grateful to be still alive. The fact that he was only a couple of days away from his beloved family was comforting. Events of the last two horrifying days ran through his mind. Questions about the next few days began to disturb him. He realized that the old man was not in the tent and, as he gazed around, he found nothing out of the ordinary. Unconsciously, he found himself uttering aloud, "I must leave this place. I must be out of here!"

From outside, the slit on the side of the entrance to the tent was pushed open as the old Bedouin peeked in and then said cautiously, "Your mule is waiting out there with enough food and water for the road. All seems under control in the city. No more robbing and killing. They've got them all, at least for now. But I really don't know about the Mamelukes in Upper Egypt and other places."

"Well, thanks for the mule and the food. I believe that I should make my move now and get on the road before the city gates close."

"I know how eager you are to join your family. If I may suggest, you should wait till morning."

"Had I had any chance, I would've killed Mohammed Ali without any hesitation and sent him to the gates of hell. He massacred all my friends."

"Vengeance and anger at this stage won't help in any way. Your family is the one and only thing to consider now. As you know, the city gates will open at sunrise and there'll be a lot of people going out and coming in. With the mule and my old clothes, you'll have no trouble crossing the gate tomorrow. I assure you," said the old man.

"Hag Abu Ragab! Hag Abu Ragab!"

A shout came from outside the tent. The old Bedouin motioned to Zafaran *Bey* to remain quiet as he left the tent then replied, "Who would be calling on me now?"

For a good while, he talked to another man and returned inside.

"My neighbour has brought some hay for the mule. I told him that I found it astray and I plan to feed it well before selling it."

With a faint smile, the old Bedouin spread a towel on the ground and then placed bread, goat cheese, and some tomatoes on it. Cheerfully and quietly, they ate together.

28

How could it all have been such a clever and wicked deception? How could we all have fallen into it? What did the Mamelukes really do to deserve such a gruesome, backstabbing end? What kind of a man is he really? Was it him, his soldiers or all of them? Would the infidel Napoleon have done such a deplorable thing? How safe are we under the Pasha's rule? Would he do that to us all someday? Can we believe or trust him?

These questions became the theme of discussion among the people of Cairo who were certainly not expecting or demanding any answers. Rather, it seemed like a way of expressing their predicament and fear. Despite many centuries of obvious discontent with the Mamelukes, Egyptians were saddened and morally injured.

The old Bedouin and Zafaran *Bey* started their day early. Again, they had bread, goat cheese, dried dates, and water for breakfast. It was clear that the shooting and looting had stopped and that life in the city seemed somewhat normal. Heading towards the western gate, while dragging the mule through poor districts, they blended perfectly with the population. Though grief appeared visible on many faces, poor districts were not as affected as much by the deeds committed by the brutal soldiers. Dust, stench, and noise filled the air and dirt could be found at every corner. Occasionally, they encountered on their way many volunteers carrying coffins of innocent victims to burial grounds. As they approached the western gate, crowds suddenly multiplied and the old Bedouin said, "We couldn't have asked for better timing. God be with you, son!"

He then handed the cheap harness of the mule to Zafaran *Bey,* embraced him, and shook his hands. By now it was a known fact that thousands of the Mamelukes, who lived in Cairo and nearby regions, had been slaughtered and that several army units had been dispatched all over the country to slay the rest. Nevertheless, soldiers thoroughly examined each passing face at the gate. The old Bedouin could not evade the soldiers' searching eyes; however, an idea struck him.

"Look here! Let me pretend to be your father. I'll ride the mule and you walk ahead with your face to the ground while gently pulling the harness," he suggested to Zafaran *Bey.*

"Don't you have to meet some people tomorrow?"

"I can always return after you cross the gate. Clearly, you look distinctly like a Bedouin but they may suspect you if you're alone. Please! Don't argue with me on that one."

Zafaran *Bey* smiled and replied obediently, "Very well, dear father."

The sun was spreading its warmth all over while dust clouds were rising over the edges of the city walls. When they were a minute away from the gate, the shriek of a desperate woman began to deafen their ears.

"Mustapha, where are you? My beloved son, where are you? Who stole my son, my only son?"

Other sympathetic women began joining her in calling and searching for the lost boy. In a few minutes, the gate was virtually in disarray by the sound of wailing women. While the attention of soldiers was focused on the desperate cries, the old

Bedouin literally pushed Zafaran *Bey* through. In a steady and unhurried pace, they left the city walls unnoticed among the many other travellers and merchants. At the outskirts of the first village, the old Bedouin stopped and dismounted the mule.

"Thank God! May Allah be praised! We're through without detection. Now, I can wish you a safe trip and a happy reunion with your family. As you know, the encampment isn't far. You may get there by about this time tomorrow, if not earlier. Take care of your injuries. Some are still fresh. You have enough material to bandage them, if needed. Greet Salama for me and may God be with you!"

"Thank you for saving my life and thank you also for your great hospitality and care. May God be with us!"

Slowly, Zafaran *Bey* mounted the mule and headed towards the Western Sahara.

Epilogue

Zafaran *Bey* had a glimpse of a Bedouin encampment on the horizon at dawn. Although many palm trees obstructed his view, it took a few paces forward to recognize the camp grounds of Salama's tribe. On his mule for almost a full day, Zafaran *Bey* was nearing total exhaustion. What kept energizing his failing body was his desire to see his wife and children. Their images had strengthened his resolve and kept him on course regardless of conditions and distance. Once near the first tent, he heard dogs bark and saw a few children approach. Among them was an elder with a sword. He then knew that he had reached his destination. Every part of his body became calm and tranquil. When he glanced at the half moon and fading stars up above him, it all seemed like new. Suddenly, his memory shifted back in time. He remembered leaping off the courtyard of the Citadel, and how miraculously his stallion had saved his life. He then collapsed unconsciously to the ground.

*****

Using the same caravan with which he had entered Cairo a few weeks earlier, Mahroos happily crossed the city gate. A sense of delight and freedom overwhelmed him. His thoughts shifted between Carole and Seaham and he wondered if he would ever see either of them again. He was absolutely relieved as no one had suspected throughout his journey that he had been carrying a sack containing his newly acquired wealth. He looked forward to being back with his family and promised himself never, ever to venture again with Awaad. Though he loved Cairo, he was neither happy nor sad to leave it. In the back of his mind, he was absolutely convinced that Cairo held some incredible hidden mysteries that made so many do just about anything to return to it.

*****

Although the Mamelukes arrived in Egypt as young boys who had been purchased as slaves, they became a part of the ruling elite of warriors and regarded Egypt as their adopting country. Indeed, they ruled the region vigorously and proudly demonstrated their dexterity, ultimately creating their own history over many centuries.

The Mamelukes of Cairo and Upper Egypt reached their demise on that fateful day when the Massacre at the Citadel eliminated almost all of these proud soldiers. The remaining Mamelukes, who had managed to escape beyond the cataracts of the Nile into the Sudan, were pursued by military troops led by Mohammed Ali's other son, Ibrahim Pasha.

*****

Mohammed Ali was born in Kavala to Albanian parents and was raised by his uncle following the early death of his father. He enlisted in the army and became a second commander. He then joined the volunteer contingent that was sent by the

Ottoman Sultan to re-occupy Egypt following the withdrawal of Napoleon's army. Naturally, the French departure created an opportunity that led to clashes between the Ottoman forces and the Mamelukes. Mohammed Ali took advantage of the turmoil and cleverly used his loyal Albanian troops to gain power and prestige for his personal interests. Following his appointment as a governor, he plotted the massacre of the Mamelukes so he could rule Egypt freely.

Power, authority, and possession of the country characterized Mohammed Ali's ambition. After the demise of the Mamelukes, he actually regarded Egypt and its population as his personal and private domain. Nevertheless, his relentless, personal pursuit for control and domination paved the way for the development of Egypt as a modern country. His unyielding aspirations led him to occupy the Sudan, Syria, and he even attempted to march towards Constantinople. Mohammad Ali had established a great dynasty that lasted for nearly one hundred and fifty years. The last of his descendents to rule Egypt was King Farouk, who was forced to abdicate by a revolution in July 1952. Mohammad Ali died in Alexandria on August 2, 1849 and was buried, of all places, at the Citadel.

Also by the author

French Kisses on the Nile

French Kisses on the Nile takes you on a mysterious voyage beyond time and place. Enjoy being at the top of the largest pyramid in the world watching a dazzling harem from *The Thousand and One Nights* perform their seductive dances. Envision Napoleon's army roaming the streets of Cairo after their initial victory. Become a witness to an unprecedented historical encounter between Egypt and France. Discover how the two diverse cultures perceive one another during a spectacular human drama.

Beware! When the aroma of strong coffee, the haze of tobacco smoke, and the exotic perfume of stunning dancers intermingle, the outcome can never be predicted.

Available at:
Lulu.com
Amazon.com
Amazon.ca
Barnes&Noble.com
and others

eBooks:
Kindle
ibookstore
Nook Book

www.ingramcontent.com/pod-product-compliance
Lightning Source LLC
Chambersburg PA
CBHW020440180626
46812CB00003B/1329